SLAY BELLS

and

SATCHELS

A Haley Randolph Novel

Books by Dorothy Howell

HANDBAGS AND HOMICIDE

PURSES AND POISON

SHOULDER BAGS AND SHOOTINGS

CLUTCHES AND CURSES

TOTE BAGS AND TOE TAGS

Slay Bells

and

Satchels

By Dorothy Howell

DH

www.DorothyHowellNovels.com

ISBN: 978-0-9856930-0-8

With Love to David, Stacy, Judy, Seth and Brian

ACKNOWLEDGEMENTS

This author is eternally grateful to everyone who generously gave their time, effort, and support to the creation of this book. Some of them are: Judith Branstetter, David Howell, Stacy Howell, Evie Cook, and William F. Wu Ph.D.

Chapter 1

"Ho-ho-Holt's for the holidays!" everyone in the training room shouted.

Everyone but me, that is.

There's only so much I'll do for a lousy eight bucks an hour.

Yet here I was stuck in another coma-inducing training session at Holt's Department Store. I'd taken my usual spot—the last row behind that big guy who works in Men's Wear—where my eyes could glaze over unnoticed.

This meeting was for the kick-off for today's annual Summer Santa Sale. All kinds of special things were planned. We employees had already been subjected to several of these meetings over the past few weeks, where details of the event had been discussed.

At least that's what somebody told me. I'd drifted off.

That happens a lot.

Luckily, my crappy sales clerk job here at the equally crappy Holt's Department Store wasn't the sum total of my existence.

I, Haley Randolph, with my I'm-tall-enough-to-model-but-I-don't five foot nine inch height, my I-could-be-in-a-shampoo-commercial-but-I'm-not dark hair, and my beauty queen genes—yeah, okay, it's only half of them—had a really great life, despite my current employer.

Honestly, my job situation had always been … well, to be generous I'll say sporadic—which was totally not my fault. I swear. It's just that I haven't found my niche yet.

But I've tried. At the age of twenty four—which was starting to scare me because, oh my God, thirty wasn't that far away—I'd already worked as a life guard, file clerk, receptionist, and two unfortunate weeks at a pet store. I thought I'd hit the job lottery last fall when I went to work for the all-powerful, all-knowing Pike Warner law firm. But then there was that whole administrative-leave-investigation-pending thing—long story.

I was also pursuing my B.A.—at least, that's what it said on my résumé. I didn't like college. It seemed a lot like high school all over again, except nobody cared what you wore.

So as not to overwhelm myself, I took no more than two classes per semester. My grades had been good, thanks to my awesome cut-and-paste skills, and because I have the uncanny ability to choose a seat near a smart person who doesn't cover their paper.

It's a gift, really.

But now it was summer and that meant—yeah!—I wasn't slogging my way through some dull, boring college class. My best friend Marcie Hanover and I were giving killer purse parties and raking in the cash. I had a fabulous apartment in Santa Clarita—about thirty minutes north of Los Angeles, depending on traffic—that I adored. Ty Cameron—he's way hot—was still my official boyfriend.

At least he was the last time I heard from him, whenever that was.

Ty's ancestors founded the Holt's department store chain back in the day. Yes, it was the same Holt's where I worked as a sales clerk—long story. He was the fifth generation of his family to be totally obsessed and out of his mind consumed with running the business to the exclusion of all else.

Nobody seemed to understand why Ty and I were dating—including me. Months passed before we did the deed and became official boyfriend-girlfriend. He said he was crazy about me. I could stand to hear some specifics but he hasn't given any—not that he's really tried.

I was crazy about him, too. The only specifics I could come up with were that he's handsome, successful, and looked great in an

Armani suit—which made me sound kind of shallow. I'm not. There was something deep going on between us. I just didn't know what it was.

Ty seemed to think we had an *understanding* about his job.

He would be wrong.

The only *understanding* I had was that if we had a date, he should actually show up—on time would be nice—and not spend the entire evening texting and blabbing on the phone about yet another problem at Holt's.

Was that too much to ask?

Apparently, it was.

And, apparently, it was too much to hope that this butt-numbing Summer Santa Sale meeting would end soon. I mean, jeez, it wasn't like we hadn't heard all of this info before—or that any of us actually cared about it in the first place.

During a few lucid moments in previous meetings, I'd learned that this sale was a huge event previewing the upcoming holiday merchandise at super low prices—I figured it was really just a way to get rid of all the crappy Christmas merchandise that didn't sell last year, but hey, that's just me.

This morning everyone had reported for work an hour before the store opened to attend this one last somebody-please-kill-me-now meeting. The sale was a huge deal—to management, who had compensation packages, that is—and everyone up the corporate ladder was anxious to max out their bonus, courtesy of our hard work.

Although, as Jeanette, our store manager, had pointed out on numerous occasions, this time there was indeed something in it for the rest of us. A contest for the employees also kicked off today.

We sales clerks were supposed to hunt down customers in the store—yeah, like we were really going to do that—or accost them—my words, not management's—while they were trapped in the checkout line, and ask them to make a monetary donation that

Holt's would use to buy toys for underprivileged children when Christmas actually rolled around.

We'd been given little booklets with Christmas trees printed on them along with bar codes that would register their donation at checkout.   In turn, customers would receive a discount on their orders.   The store in the Holt's chain that collected the most donations won a prize.

Or something like that.   I don't know.   The whole spiel had turned into blah, blah, blah every time Jeanette explained it.

"One more time!" someone shouted, jarring me out of a perfectly good daydream.

I hate it when that happens.

The daydream was about an insanely fabulous handbag I'd found in *Elle* magazine last night.   It was the Breathless, a satchel constructed by vision-impaired Italian artisans using only their highly developed sense of touch to select buttery leathers, richly textured fabrics, and multi-faceted crystals, while working only on national holidays, wearing velvet capes passed down from their ancestors living in seclusion high in the Andes Mountains—or something like that. I don't know. Maybe I'm getting that confused with the movie I was watching just before I fell asleep. Anyway, the Breathless was an awesome handbag and I absolutely had to have one.

At the front of the room Jeanette raised her arms, indicating that all the employees should stand. We clamored to our feet.

Not to be unkind, but Jeanette had put on a little weight lately that had all settled around her middle. She was in her fifties so I guess she either thought that was okay, or in her head she was twenty years younger and forty pounds lighter.

The really troubling part was that Jeanette insisted on dressing in Holt's women's wear. Don't ask me why. She made major bucks and could afford really nice things.

No way anyone with enough good taste to so much as glance at the cover of *Vogue* magazine while standing in the grocery checkout line would think Holt's clothing should actually be worn and not sent immediately to the recycle bin.

Honestly, shouldn't there be some law against Holt's filling their racks with these hideous clothes and having them lie in wait for unsuspecting customers? Where were the fashion police when you needed them?

In what I could only hope was a nod to today's launch of the Christmas-themed sales event and not a preview of fashions to come, Jeanette had on a white two-piece suit accessorized for no known reason with large black buttons up the front.

She looked like a snowman on steroids.

"Everybody! Let's hear it!" Jeanette shouted. "Ho-ho-Holt's for the holidays!"

The employees cheered along with her, just as if we gave a rip one way or the other that the sale was a success, and weren't doing it because we needed to keep our jobs.

"Now let's get out there and have a super Summer Santa Sale!" Jeanette said, our cue that it was time to get to work.

Since it was my personal policy to always be the last person to enter the training room for a meeting, I compensated for this by being the first one out the door. Bella, my Holt's BFF, fell in beside me.

Bella was about my age, tall, coffee to my cream. She'd worked here longer than me and didn't like it either—thus, our close friendship—but she was sticking it out to save for beauty school.

Bella's goal was to design hairstyles for the rich and famous. In the meantime, she practiced on her own hair. I guessed she was going with a Christmas theme, in keeping with the Summer Santa Sale, because this morning she'd styled what I was sure was a wreath atop her head.

The red bow gave it away.

"It's b.s.," Bella grumbled. "You ask me, it's b.s."

Standing in the doorway was Colleen, one of the sales clerks. To be generous, I'll call her *slow*—and believe me, I'm being *way* generous.

"Happy holidays," she said, and held out two Santa hats, the red ones with the white fake-fur band and fuzzy ball on top.

Bella and I froze in front of her.

Was there no end to the humiliation minimum wage employees must endure?

"It's a hat," Colleen said. "You put it on your head."

See?

"It's b.s.," Bella snarled. "That's what it is. It's b.s."

She snatched the hat out of Colleen's hand and moved on. I did the same.

"I am not putting that thing on my head," Bella declared, as we walked down the corridor toward the sales floor.

I was with Bella on this one. No way was I dealing with hat-hair—not even if I got an upper management salary package.

That's how I roll.

We headed through the store to our assigned corners of retail purgatory—today, it was the Domestics Department for me, Children's Wear for Bella—and I had to admit the store looked great. The display team had gone all out turning the store into a holiday wonderland in an attempt to evoke feelings of home, hearth, and family, thereby playing on our customers' emotions in an effort to wring a few more bucks out of them.

In the center aisle was a line of towering Christmas trees, each fully lighted and decorated to the hilt, guarded by a small army of three-foot-tall wooden soldiers. Swags of garland hung from the ceiling, along with wreaths, stockings, and thick red ribbon.

Nearby were display shelves filled with boxed ornaments, tree skirts, lights, and garland. Nativity scenes, angels, and nutcrackers sat on another shelving unit. Another display held gift bows, wrapping paper, and greeting cards. Boxes of candy, nuts, and peppermints—jeez, I really hope that stuff's not left from last year—and bottles of Bolt, the Holt's house brand energy drink, were positioned close by.

Through the big plate glass doors at the entrance, I saw about two dozen customers already waiting for the store to open. A number of them wore full-on Santa costumes—red suits and hats, black boots, and long white beards.

"What's with the outfits?" I asked.

"Part of the sale," Bella said. "Wear the suit, get a fifty-percent discount."

Nice to know we employees weren't the only ones Holt's subjected to total humiliation.

"Haley?" someone called.

Thinking that somehow a customer had slipped into the store early and needed my help, I started walking away faster.

"Haley!"

Now I recognized the voice. It was Jeanette. All the more reason to feign ignorance and stride away quickly, but I figured she'd just continue to pursue me.

I'm pretty sure they covered that in the Holt's management training course.

I stopped and waited while she caught up to me.

"Haley, Rita won't be in today," Jeanette said, panting slightly.

This boosted my day considerably. Rita was the cashier's supervisor.

I hate Rita.

I could only hope she had some sort of drug resistant staff infection—call it my little Christmas wish.

"I need you to take over for her," Jeanette said.

In keeping with my own personal say-no-to-additional-duties policy, I said, "I can't do that, Jeanette."

Apparently, Jeanette had her own ignore-employees-who-claim-they-can't-take-on-additional-duties policy.

"You'll have to be the elf wrangler today," she said.

She wanted me to be the—what?

Jeanette nodded toward the rear of the store. "They're getting ready in the assistant manager's office."

There were elves in the store, getting ready for something?

Maybe I should start paying attention in the meetings.

Jeanette glanced at her watch. "We're opening in eleven minutes. Those girls have to be in costume, hair and makeup done, and in place to greet the customers when the doors open."

I had no idea what the heck she was talking about, so what could I say but, "Okay."

"I told Corporate that hiring actresses this year was a bad idea. First day on the job and they're already running late." She huffed irritably. "You'll have to supervise the contest entries and the drawings."

There was a contest and a drawing?

Jeez, you space-out in a couple of meetings and you miss all kinds of stuff.

Jeanette gestured to the front of the store. Near the entrance on a little platform sat a full-sized, heavy cardboard fireplace, complete with stockings. A decorated Christmas tree sat next to it, alongside a big green hopper. The display was surrounded by red velvet ropes held up by huge candy canes.

Where did that come from?

"Be sure there's always an elf standing there to greet the customers and have them fill out an entry form," Jeanette said. "A winner has to be drawn every hour, on the hour, so make sure one of the elves is in place. The rest of them will circulate through the store asking for donations for the children's charity."

Jeanette didn't wait for me to say anything—which was probably wise on her part. She turned to leave, but stopped immediately.

"Thank goodness," she mumbled. "Here they come."

Down the aisle came a bunch of young, pretty girls, all of them decked out in elf costumes. I guessed they were all in their early twenties, differing in heights, but not a size larger than a six among them. They wore green shorts and vests over red and white striped tights and long-sleeved tops, and green, pointed-toed elf shoes. Everyone had on a Santa hat, bright red lipstick, and big circles of pink blush on their cheeks.

"Good, we're all set," Jeanette said, taking one last look around. "When the customers come in—"

She stopped abruptly and her gaze drilled into me.

"Where's the giant toy bag?" she demanded.

The giant—what?

"The giant toy bag is supposed to be right next to the fireplace," Jeanette declared. "It must still be in the stockroom. Get it, Haley. It *has* to be in place when the customers come in."

I headed for the rear of the store, pausing only long enough to ditch my Santa hat behind a display of T-shirts. The entrance to the stockroom—one of them, anyway—was located beside the customer service booth near the hallway that led to the employee break room, the training room, and the store managers' offices.

I went through the swinging door into the stockroom. It was as quiet as an evening snowfall back here. Unless the truck team was on duty unloading a big rig filled with new merchandise, nobody came in here often. The rear door by the loading dock was propped open for the janitor. The store's music track played "Jingle Bells."

I spotted a red toy bag right away. It was a giant, all right, just as Jeanette had said. It sat on the floor in front of the huge shelving unit that held the store's entire inventory of Christmas decorations.

Half the contents of one of the shelves was scattered on the floor, which was weird, but I didn't have time to clean it up. I'd come back and do it later—not that I was all that concerned about maintaining a neat, orderly stockroom, but I never passed up a chance to escape the sales floor.

I grabbed the bag. Yikes! It wouldn't budge.

I pulled it again using two hands. It moved maybe a couple of inches.

Jeez, this thing weighed a ton.

No way could I carry it to the front of the store, and dragging it would take forever. Even loading it onto one of the long, thin U-boat carts we used to transport merchandise wouldn't be easy.

There was nothing to do but take out some of the toys.

I pulled open the draw string closure at the top of the bag and—

Oh my God. *Oh my God.*

There was an elf inside.

Dead.

Chapter 2

"There's a dead elf in the stockroom," I said.

Jeanette didn't look frightened, alarmed, or worried, just annoyed—at me. Like it was my fault, or something.

"I already called 9-1-1," I said.

She huffed, pulled out her cell phone and started punching buttons calling, I was sure, the corporate office.

We'd been through this before—long story—so we both knew the drill.

The elves—all nine of them—were gathered near the fireplace. A few of them were waving to the customers waiting outside, some were talking to each other, most were checking themselves out in the mirrors by the Sportswear Department.

"Excuse me," I called, using my there's-nothing-to-be-alarmed-about voice. The elves quieted down and turned to me, and I immediately launched into my you-can-trust-me voice. "Would you all come with me, please?"

I turned and walked away. With men, I found this always worked. Men followed, no matter what. Not so with women.

I glanced back and saw the elves still clustered by the fireplace, whispering and giving each other questioning looks.

"Just a change of plans," I said, using my it's-no-big-deal voice.

It was an outright lie, of course, but what else could I do? I had to get the elves sequestered in the training room so the homicide detectives could question them.

I motioned for them to follow and they did. I led them to the training room in the back of the store.

"The store manager will be here in a few minutes," I told them.

I intended to make my escape and let Jeanette break the news—I'm sure that was covered in her Holt's management training course, well, pretty sure—so I headed for the door.

"Somebody's missing," an elf called.

I turned back and saw one of the girls doing a head count.

"There're only nine of us," she said. "Someone's not here."

Miss Helpful. Great. Thank you so much.

"It's McKenna," someone else said. "McKenna's not here."

"She's probably setting up interviews for her personal assistant," someone else said, in a snarky voice.

A few of the girls laughed.

Someone else said, "Or maybe she's shopping for her beach condo."

"Bitch," another girl murmured.

Jeanette appeared. No way did I want to be around when she broke the news to the girls. I closed the door and headed for the break room.

The chocolate in the vending machines called to me—yes, actually called. It's never too early in the day to have a Snickers bar, and since I'd just discovered a dead body at my crappier-than-crappy part-time job, I saw no reason not to heed its sirens song.

Still, maybe it could wait a couple of minutes.

I'd called 9-1-1 from the stockroom as soon as I'd found the dead elf in the toy bag—we're not supposed to keep our cell phones on us during duty hours, but we're not supposed to keep a dead elf in the stockroom either. I knew the cops, detectives, and crime scene investigators would show up soon. I decided to take another look around before they got there.

I don't have professional training, of course, but I do have mad Scooby Doo skills. Besides, I'd already been in there once, so I figured I couldn't screw up the crime scene if I went back.

I glanced up and down the hallway, saw that no one was around, and slipped into the stockroom.

The giant toy bag lay just where I left it. It creeped me out looking at it.

Scattered across the floor and piled up nearby were the Christmas decorations that had been knocked off the shelving unit. Some of the glass ornaments were broken. Yards of green garland and dozens of spools of red ribbon were jumbled in with a mound of wooden nutcrackers, the ones that look like soldiers with gaping mouths.

Those things creep me out, too.

I figured that McKenna—I guess she was the victim since the other elves had said she was missing from the training room—had struggled with her attacker and knocked everything onto the floor.

Her assailant must have emptied the contents of the giant toy bag and stuffed her inside, after the deed was done. Small household and kitchen appliances, electric razors and toothbrushes, holiday placemat and napkins sets—apparently, Holt's had planned to give away "toys" to all ages—were mixed with teddy bears, coloring books and crayons, and wooden puzzles, and dumped on top of the Christmas decorations.

Obviously, McKenna's death wasn't an accident or suicide— you don't need mad skills to know she hadn't offed herself, then crawled into the giant toy bag to die—and that meant she'd been murdered.

I got a really creepy feeling.

I looked around. The loading bay doors were still closed. The back door I'd thought the janitor had opened was still open. No sign of the janitor.

I spotted a puddle of blood seeping from under a pile of large, wooden candy canes.

Yuck. I wanted out of there.

I headed for the door.

 It burst open in front of me.

Homicide detectives Madison and Shuman walked in.

Oh, crap.

"Leaving the scene of the crime, I see, Miss Randolph," Detective Madison said, looking smug. "Seems I'm getting an early Christmas present this year."

Detective Madison hated me. But that's okay. I hated him, too.

He was way overdue for retirement, and looked it. His comb-over had thinned even more and his jowls hung lower than the last time I saw him. He had a round belly that definitely shook when he laughed like a bowl full of jelly—not that he ever laughed, around me, anyway. Madison had made it his mission to find me guilty of *something*.

Detective Shuman didn't hate me. I didn't hate him, either.

He was thirtyish, with brown hair, and kind of handsome—not that I ever noticed, of course, since I have an official boyfriend. Shuman had an official girlfriend that he absolutely adored. So, officially, there was nothing going on between Shuman and me. Officially.

"I'll leave you two to your work," I said, and skirted around the detectives.

Madison blocked my path.

"Oh, no, let's get to the good stuff, like opening the biggest present first on Christmas morning," he said, rubbing his palms together. "You were in charge of the actresses who were portraying elves here today, weren't you?"

I guess he'd already talked to Jeanette.

"Well, yes," I said. "But that only happened this morning, just a short while ago, really."

"So it was a crime of opportunity," Madison said. "Is that what you're telling me, Miss Randolph?"

"No," I insisted.

"So what sort of crime was it?" he asked, leaning closer.

I glanced at Shuman. He looked worried.

Not good.

"I had nothing to do with McKenna's murder," I said.

Madison snapped to attention, as if I'd just confessed to something.

"So you knew the victim," he declared.

"No, I just heard the other girls talking about her," I told him.

He went on as if I hadn't spoken.

"And you knew she'd been *murdered*," he declared.

Well, I guess he had me on that.

"You supposedly *found* the body," Madison went on. "You *found* her when you were *alone* in the stockroom. Isn't that right, Miss Randolph?"

Okay, he had me on that, too.

But he was making it sound as if I'd actually done something wrong.

"I didn't kill her," I insisted.

Detective Madison narrowed his beady little eyes at me until they almost disappeared, and leaned closer.

"We'll find out," he said. Madison jerked his thumb toward the door. "You can go now."

I was glad to leave, but a little miffed at being dismissed. Still, I didn't want to hang around and see McKenna's body when the investigators from the coroner's office showed up and pulled her out of the bag.

I brushed past the detectives.

"Don't leave town, Miss Randolph," Detective Madison called.

I pushed through the stockroom door without answering.

I took a lap through the store just to burn off the negative energy Detective Madison had left me with. I was supposed to work in the Domestics Department today, but no way could I face that right now.

The aisles were crowded with shoppers, a couple of babies were crying, some lady was yelling at her husband—why on earth do women take their husbands shopping with them?—and a group of teenage girls was swarming the lingerie department like locusts in a Kansas wheat field.

Everybody seemed to be in the Christmas spirit—spending-wise, at least. Lots of people had full carts, others juggled items in their arms. I spotted several customers in Santa costumes.

Apparently, public humiliation wasn't too high a price for some people to pay when a huge discount was dangled in front of them.

Nobody, it seemed, knew that an elf had been murdered in the stockroom. Hopefully, it wouldn't make the news. Holt's had a good PR department and knew how to handle this sort of thing—believe me, I know. I'd heard Ty talking to them often enough during one of our supposed dates.

At the front of the store I spotted Sandy standing beside the fake fireplace wearing a Holt's-issued Santa hat. Sandy was another of my Holt's BFFs. She was in her early twenties, a white girl with red hair that she usually wore in a ponytail. Sandy was super nice—so nice that when her boyfriend—he's a tattoo artist she met on the Internet—treated her like crap—which was almost all the time—she didn't even notice.

A few customers had gathered outside the red velvet ropes that cordoned off the fireplace and others were busy filling out contest entry forms at the little tables set up nearby. I circled around to the back of the display so the customers wouldn't overhear.

"What's going on?" I asked Sandy. "Where are the elves?"

"Jeanette told me to run the drawing," Sandy said. "The elves were completely traumatized by the news. I guess they all know each other."

I wondered if they knew that girl who used to work here at Holt's—I can never remember her name—the one who used to stink up the break room with her diet meals. She'd lost eighty pounds, or something, gone blonde, swapped her glasses for contacts, and gotten an agent. Last I heard she was doing really great, modeling for print ads.

I hate her, of course.

"So, anyway," Sandy said, "Jeanette let them have the day off—with pay."

"With—what?"

How come I didn't get the day off—with pay? I'd found the dead elf. Didn't she think I might be traumatized, too?

More likely Jeanette figured the elves might sue Holt's and I wouldn't.

Neither Ty nor I had ever come right out and told Jeanette we were dating, but I'm sure she knew—long story. Ty preferred to keep his personal life quiet, which was understandable, but I didn't see any reason why I shouldn't get some preferential treatment around here out of the deal.

"Are the elves coming back tomorrow?" I asked Sandy.

She shrugged. "I don't know. Most of them were really upset about what happened. They were afraid."

I doubted some whack-job, psycho elf murderer was on the loose, but you never knew. This was, after all, L.A.

"And you know what this means for our contest," Sandy said.

There was a contest?

"All the employees are really excited about winning a big prize," she said.

Then I remembered that we were supposed to hit up customers for a donation to the children's Christmas toy charity drive, and that the store that collected the most money won a prize.

"Without those elves here, I don't know if we have a chance of winning," Sandy said. "I wish you hadn't told everybody about that dead elf in the stockroom."

"What was I supposed to do? *Leave* her there?"

Sandy shook her head. "Some of the employees think you blew our chances of pulling off a big win."

"The prizes were probably really lame, anyway," I said.

"Still," Sandy said. "I'm just saying."

"Whatever. I've got to go," I said.

I headed through the store again in the general direction of the Domestics Department, but was in no rush to actually report there, or do any actual work.

I thought I'd done enough for Holt's today.

Since Jeanette and most of the department managers were probably still in the offices dealing with the police investigation, I saw no reason not to take full advantage of the situation.

I walked to the Shoe Department, careful—as always—to keep my eyes straight forward and move at a rapid pace to discourage customers from attempting to stop me and ask for help. I hurried between the racks of shoes, and slipped into the stockroom.

The Shoe Department had its own stockroom. Since the shelves had to be replenished so often, management didn't want employees abandoning the sales floor for long periods of time to fetch shoes from the big stockroom at the back of the store.

I guess they thought some employees might take advantage of the situation and just hang out in there. I mean, really, *who* would do such a thing?

Anyway, the Shoe Department stockroom was filled with shelves of shoes, of course, but it also had a little desk, chair and telephone for the department manager to use.

Like management didn't think anyone would take advantage of those things?

Inside the stockroom, I closed the door, dropped into the desk chair, and whipped out my cell phone.

My day needed a boost. So what could lift my spirits better than talking to my official boyfriend?

I punched in Ty's number, my mind filling with the image of him.

At this time of day he would be at the Holt's corporate headquarters in downtown Los Angeles. He'd be wearing one of his expensive suits with a perfectly coordinated shirt and tie, his light brown hair combed carefully into place. He'd be sitting at his ridiculously overpriced desk, in his bigger-than-most-two-bedroom-apartments office, with an amazing view that jacked up the price of the building to equal the gross national product of most South American countries. He'd be making decisions that involved millions of dollars and affected the lives of thousands of people. He'd see my name on his caller I.D. screen. He'd stop everything. All the problems facing Holt's would have to come to a standstill because I was calling. He'd answer on the first ring because he would be so thrilled to talk to me.

Just before the sixth ring when his voicemail would pick up—I know this because I'd heard his phone ring a few billion times—Ty answered.

"Yeah?" he said.

"Hi," I said. "How's your morning?"

"What? Hang on." I heard him talking to someone in the background, then he came back on the line. "Haley? Yeah, what's up?"

"Nothing," I said. "I just had a rough morning and I wanted to—"

"Hang on." Ty spoke to someone for a minute or so, then came back to me. "I heard what happened this morning."

I doubted he'd heard that I'd found the body, or that my old nemesis Detective Madison was on the case and had already decided I was a suspect.

I saw no reason to tell Ty those things.

"P.R. already has a lid on it," Ty said. "I don't think it will affect sales."

"You're being a really crappy boyfriend right now," I told him.

Ty went silent. I pictured him frozen in place, thinking, analyzing what I'd said, trying to determine whether I was right or wrong, and envisioning what the ramifications of taking each side of the issue would mean to our future—mostly, because Ty was definitely a male, whether this would impact how soon I'd have sex with him again.

Ty's no dummy. He came to his decision in about three seconds.

"You really had a rough morning, babe," he said. "The whole thing must have been terribly upsetting. I hate you had to go through that. You shouldn't be exposed to that sort of thing."

"You could ease my troubles by taking me out to dinner tonight," I offered.

"Oh."

I guess that was my answer.

"I'm heading to New York," Ty said, shifting into business mode again.

"Now?" I asked.

"Something came up," he said.   I heard voices in the background again, and things being shuffled around. "I'll only be there a couple of days. When I come back I'll take you any place you'd like. I promise."

"You're *really* being a crappy boyfriend right now," I said.

"Yes, I know, and I'm sorry," Ty said. "But I'll make it up to you. I swear."

"You'd better," I told him.

"I will. I'll talk to you later," he said, and hung up.

I rose from the chair and shoved my cell phone into my pocket. Crap. So much for my day getting a boost.

I couldn't help but notice that Ty hadn't asked me to accompany him to New York. I'd been to Europe with him on a business trip— long story—and, surprise-surprise, he was no fun. Still, it would have been nice to be invited, and with a murder investigation underway and me a sort-of suspect, it would be a great time for me to leave town.

Another more depressing thought flew into my head.

What if Ty had already spoken to the homicide detectives? What if he knew I was a suspect? Could that have been why he left town so suddenly? And didn't ask me to go with him?

Not a great feeling.

I wasn't quite up to facing the Domestics Department yet, but since the cops were probably still in the main stockroom, and everybody knew to look for me in the break room—my all-time favorite hiding place—I figured I'd just hang out in here for a while. Maybe I'd give Marcie a call and see what was up with our next purse party, or schedule a mani and pedi for myself—that would improve my day.

My cell phone buzzed.

My heart jumped. Was it Ty? Had he cancelled his New York trip? Had it just occurred to him that he should have invited me to go with him? Was he on his way here to sweep me off of my feet?

I yanked my phone from my pocket and read the name on the caller I.D. screen. I gasped aloud and my heart thudded against my ribcage.

Oh my God. Jack Bishop was calling.

Jack was a super-hot private detective. I met him last fall when I'd worked at the law firm of Pike Warner—long story. He still worked there doing investigations—all of which just *had* to be really cool—and also took some cases on the side.

He had gorgeous dark hair, deep blue eyes, and a fantastic build. We've traded favors—strictly professional, of course—for the past few months, helping each other out with investigations.

"I'm dealing with a pressing situation," Jack said when I answered.

He spoke in his Barry White voice, the one that made my stomach feel hot and gooey, and my toes curl.

"Would you call this a problem?" I asked.

"A big one," he said. "A very big one. I'd like to share it with you."

I tried to say something, but I couldn't seem to form a complete sentence.

"I need relief, Haley," Jack said. "And you—only you—have the necessary, shall we say, unique abilities to relieve this pressing situation."

Oh my God. I collapsed into the desk chair.

"Meet me tonight at eight," Jack said. "Wear something short."

Chapter 3

I didn't wear something short.

Well, okay, it was kind of short—but it wasn't my fault. My mother was a former beauty queen. Really. Though my chromosomal line up had somehow mismatched on her beauty, poise, and any-actual-talent genes, I'd inherited her long pageant legs. So skirts that were a normal length on most everybody else were super short on me.

I walked into the restaurant on Santa Monica Boulevard where Jack had asked me to meet him at a little after eight o'clock. The place was decorated with dark wood, faux stone, and low, amber lighting like just about every other place these days. A restaurant was on the right with big windows that looked out onto the busy street. A bar was on the left.

The girl behind the hostess stand smiled when I walked up.

"I'm meeting someone," I said.

"Jack?" she asked.

When I nodded, she looked like she might have been jealous. I couldn't be sure, but I hoped so.

She led the way into the bar.

The place wasn't exactly packed but lots of people sat on stools at the bar and at the tables surrounding it. There was no band playing or DJ bumping tunes.

I didn't really know what to expect from my meeting with Jack tonight, although all sorts of scenarios had whipped around in my head—which was bad of me, I know, especially since my official boyfriend was out of town, but there it was. Yet never in my wildest dreams—and I've have some really crazy ones—did I expect to find Jack seated at a romantic corner table with another woman.

I figured her for late twenties. Ordinary looking—attractive, but ordinary. Tired, maybe. She had on minimal makeup. Her blonde hair was pulled back in a ponytail and approximately ten days overdue for a fresh cut. She wore a simple white blouse over denim capris.

Jack looked hot—*way* hot—in jeans and a snug, green Henley shirt.

His head was leaned close to hers. She said something I couldn't hear. Jack glanced at his watch, spoke to her, and patted her arm.

I wondered if I'd wasted my totally awesome outfit, a black look-at-my-legs skirt, a dark-haired-girls-get-noticed-in-red tank top, slightly slutty heels, and a beyond gorgeous Chanel satchel.

Only one way to find out.

"Hi," I said, walking up.

Jack rose from his chair, but before he could say anything, the woman shot to her feet.

"Haley?" she asked, looking at me as if I were some long lost relative.

I glanced at Jack, then said, "Yeah, I'm Haley."

She dashed around the table and threw her arms around me.

"Thank you. Thank you for coming," she said, squeezing me. "Thank you."

I hit Jack with a what-the-heck look and he pried her off of me.

"Let's all sit down," he said.

She drew back and I saw tears standing in her eyes.

"I'm sorry," she said. "I'm just a little emotional these days."

"Haley, this is Brooke Stafford," Jack said, as we all sat down.

The waitress appeared. Jack ordered another beer; the white wine in front of Brooke looked as if it hadn't been touched.

"Just a soda," I said, since I was driving.

"Brooke's involved with a delicate situation," Jack began. "It seems—"

"My in-laws kidnapped my daughter," she blurted out.

I reeled back a little. "What?"

"They have her. They won't give her back. They claim they don't have her." Brooke's words came out in a frantic rush. Tears sprang from her eyes. "They say that if I don't have her, then she must be dead. I must have killed her!"

"It's okay," Jack said softly.

He pulled her onto his shoulder and she buried her face against his neck. After a minute or so, she sat up again and swiped at her tears.

"I'm sorry," Brooke said, sniffing.

"Brooke's husband died six months ago," Jack said. "Chris Stafford."

A jolt hit me.

"Oh, my God. You're *that* Brooke Stafford?" I asked.

The Staffords lived in a mansion on Pasadena's Orange Grove Boulevard that had been in their family for a couple of generations. I knew this because the social circle my parents traveled in often intersected that of the Staffords.

They were what my mother referred to as "old money," which meant they were not only loaded but also connected to civic, social and business leaders. None of those ties, however, saved them from the ultimate heartache when in January of this year their son Chris—their only child—had been killed in a car crash.

"Sorry about your husband," I said to Brooke.

She dabbed at the corners of her eyes, then said, "So I guess you know what it was like with Chris's parents."

I only knew what I'd heard from my mom. She was a world class gossip. If talking smack about people was an Olympic event, she'd have the gold medal.

"I heard that you weren't exactly what they had in mind for a daughter-in-law," I said.

What I'd really heard was that Brooke came from a middle class—which, in the eyes of Alton and Sable Stafford really meant low class—family who worked at middle class jobs and lived in a middle class house in a middle class neighborhood.

That alone made Brooke unworthy of their son.

"Chris's parents never accepted me," Brooke said. "I didn't want to come between them. I told him that. But, well, we loved each other. We got married. They refused to come to the ceremony. They were just awful about everything."

Like most people with money and power, Alton and Sable were used to getting what they wanted, when they wanted it. No way would they have been happy with their son's decision to marry Brooke.

"Then we had our daughter." Brooke smiled and reached for her purse. "Want to see a picture?"

"Sure," I said.

She pulled a photo from her wallet and passed it to me.

"She's four now," Brooke said, still smiling. "We named her 'Hope,' because, well, Chris and I hoped that after his parents saw her, they'd come around, be more accepting. We even bought a home—a really nice place in Culver City—with a guest house, thinking maybe they'd stay with us and spend more time with her."

The little girl in the picture looked like one of those angels you see depicted on greeting cards. She had a halo of blonde curly hair, a pink bow mouth, and huge blue eyes.

"She's a cutie pie," I said, handing the photo back to her.

Brooke stared down at the picture and her eyes filled with tears again.

"Put it away," Jack said softly and patted her arm. "We'll get her back."

Brooke nodded and tucked the picture into her purse.

The waitress appeared with our drinks. She must have picked up on the tension at our table because she dropped them and left.

"So here's where we are," Jack said, shifting into business mode. "After Chris died, Brooke did the right thing. She contacted the Staffords, offered to let bygones be bygones, and asked if they wanted to see little Hope. They did. They started visiting each other regularly. It went well, so Brooke let Hope spend the night at their house a few times. No problem."

"They then asked if they could keep her for a week," Brooke said. "I told them no, at first. A whole week? Without my baby? She's my *life*. My whole *life*. I couldn't live without her for that long. I just couldn't."

"But you changed your mind?" I asked.

Anger swept over Brooke's face, wiping away her anguish.

"I don't know why I believed them," she said, pounding her fist on the table. "But they'd been so nice—for months. They hadn't said one harsh word against me. I thought they'd really changed, that losing Chris had made them see that family was important. They said I needed a break, so they insisted I go to a spa near San Francisco to relax and rejuvenate."

I didn't need binoculars to see where this was going.

"And when you got back, they wouldn't give your daughter to you," I said.

"They claim they don't have her," Brooke said, getting wild-eyed again. "It's a lie! They have her! She's in that house!"

Jack motioned with his hand for her to settle down and said to me, "The Staffords claim they don't have the little girl. They told Brooke that if the child had been missing for a week and she hadn't reported it to the police, then Brooke must have killed the kid. They're threatening to report it to the cops."

"But she has an alibi," I pointed out. "The week at the spa."

"Oh, they lied about that, too," Brooke declared. "When I got there, they said I had no reservation. They couldn't accommodate me. So I just bummed around San Francisco for a few days."

"You still left a paper trail," I said.

Jack shook his head. "The detectives could piece together her hotels and restaurants, but they can't account for every single minute of every day and night. They could claim she did away with the child, then went up north to fabricate an alibi. They could say she took the child with her, did away with her up there. Even if Brooke could somehow avoid the charges, the damage would already be done."

I could imagine the media storm. Brooke would be branded as the worst kind of child killer. Her name and photo would be splashed all over TV, newspapers, the Internet. The legal battle would take most of whatever money Chris had left her, and could drag on for months, years even. When—and if—the charges were finally dropped, life would never be the same for her.

In the meantime, the Staffords could use their considerable wealth and power to change Hope's name, adopt her, and take her out of the country. Brooke would probably never see her daughter again.

"Are you sure she's in their house?" I asked.

"Oh, she's in there, all right," Brooke said. "I know because they won't let me in. I went there, and they've got some big ugly guy answering the door now. He won't let me talk to Alton or Sable. He threatened to call the police if I didn't leave."

"The house and grounds are crawling with security guards," Jack said. "I know the firm they work for. This all went into place the week Brooke was in San Francisco."

I'd been inside the mansion the Staffords called home. It was three stories with dozens of rooms, surrounded by a couple acres of grounds. With a private security staff on duty, the place was as secure as Fort Knox.

Brooke planted her elbows on the table and buried her face in her palms.

"I can't believe this is happening," she said. "I can't believe it."

"Everything is going to be all right," Jack said, slipping his arm around her shoulder. "You're getting your little girl back. I guarantee it."

Brooke looked up at him. I could see she wasn't completely convinced it would happen, but I guess she wanted to hang on to the possibility because she nodded and managed a brave smile.

"Go home," Jack said. "I'll be in touch."

She rose and said to me, "Thank you, Haley. Thank you so much."

Jack walked her outside. I watched through the window as he waited with her until the valet brought her car, a black BMW SUV that was a couple of years old. He kissed her cheek, put her inside, and watched until she drove away.

A moment later, he appeared at our table and sat down hard.

"Damn," he muttered, dragging his fingers through the hair at his temples. "I hate cases involving kids."

"Brooke's in a real mess," I said.

The waitress showed up again. Jack waved her off. He hadn't touched his beer and I'd forgotten all about my soda.

"You're sure about this?" I asked. "Sure she's telling the truth?"

I hated to ask because I could tell Brooke wasn't just another client. Jack was in deep on this one.

He didn't look offended.

"Brooke and I go way back," he said and shook his head. "No way would she hurt her little girl."

That was good enough for me.

"If she goes to the police and tells them her in-laws are holding her daughter, the Staffords will just deny it," I said. "They'll refuse to let the cops into their house to search."

"No judge will issue a warrant," Jack said. "Not without evidence. Not with somebody like Alton Stafford involved."

"You've got a plan," I said, because I knew he wouldn't have asked me here if he didn't.

"I've got a plan," Jack said. "And it involves you."

Oh my God. This was so fabulous. Jack and me on an investigation.

The vision flashed in my brain. The two of us dressed in black—I looked great in black. Maybe we could use night vision goggles and storm the house. No, wait. Maybe we could come in by helicopter and rappel onto the roof. I've always wanted to rappel down something.

"I need to keep this thing quiet," Jack said.

Damn.

"I don't want anything public," Jack said. "I don't want to push the Staffords into claiming Brooke killed the kid."

That certainly made sense, but wouldn't be near as much fun.

"All I need to do is prove the little girl is in the house," Jack said. "Once I have that evidence, Alton Stafford won't want publicity anymore than Brooke does. He'll buckle. He'll have to give the child back."

"The place is swarming with security guards," I said. "How are you going to get inside?"

Jack gave me a little grin.

"I'm walking through the front door," he said.

Oh my God. Jack was so hot.

"So how do I fit in?" I asked.

"Alton and Sable Stafford are hosting a charity event in their home," Jack said. "You've heard of it."

I knew immediately what Jack was talking about. My mom was all over it every year. The event was a huge deal involving several committees—which was really just an excuse for everyone to get together, write off their lunches and gossip about whoever wasn't at the table. It was staged every summer to—supposedly—raise money for charity. A different family hosted each year, giving everyone equal opportunity to show off their homes and attempt to make others jealous.

After all, what else did rich people have to do but put on parties for themselves so they could showcase their gowns and jewelry, and brag about their hedge funds, their trips and vacation homes, their kids and accomplishments?

Mom dragged my dad to this thing every year. It was a major yawner. I'd gone in the past, along with my brother and sister, until I got old enough that I could get away with simply refusing to go anymore.

Since I'd learned years ago to tune out most everything Mom said—it's a gift, really—I hadn't known the charity event would take place at the Stafford home this year.

"Gutsy," Jack said. "The Staffords having this party with the little girl right there in the house."

"More like arrogant. No way the guests will know Hope is in the house. Three stories. A maze of rooms. Nobody will even get near the nursery," I told him. "Besides, these events are scheduled years in advance. If the Staffords cancelled, it would send up a major red flag that something was wrong."

Jack nodded. I could see he was thinking, mentally working out the details of some plan.

I got an icky feeling in my stomach.

"I don't suppose this has anything to do with your asking me to wear something short tonight?" I asked, hoping against all hope that he'd say yes.

Jack gave my legs a quick glance.

"No," he admitted.

I guess he just wanted to look at my legs—which was kind of flattering, of course—but the icky feeling in my stomach got ickier.

"I need you to get me into that party," Jack said.

"Me? How?" I asked.

"I did some checking," he said. "Guess who's heading up the committee that's coordinating the guest list."

"Who?" I asked.

"Your mother."

Oh, crap.

Chapter 4

"Thanks a lot, Haley," somebody grumbled when I walked into the Holt's break room the next morning.

"Yeah, thanks," someone else groused.

I don't think either of them meant it.

All the employees in line at the time clock stared at me. A couple frowned, others gave me all-out stink-eye.

What was going on? What did I do?

I stored my purse—an awesome Coach tote—in my locker and took a moment to visualize how fabulous my new Breathless satchel would look in there once I got it. Then I was forced back to reality—I hate it when that happens—and got in line with the other employees, all of us waiting for our last couple of minutes of freedom to tick by before we clocked-in and began our four hours of indentured servitude. I heard some whispers and saw several people glaring at me.

The line moved forward and we clocked-in just as the door burst open and Rita, the cashier's supervisor—I hate her—came in. I put her age at early thirties. She had on her usual outfit—stretch pants and a knit top with a farm animal on it—which did nothing to flatter her I-love-fast-food-and-it-shows figure.

This morning she'd completed the look by wearing a Holt's-issued Santa hat. I noticed that all of the employees—except me, of course—had their hats with them.

"Okay, people, here's the deal," Rita announced.

Since she was blocking the doorway, we had no choice but to stand there and listen to her.

"We all know that *one of us* ruined everything for *the rest of us* yesterday," Rita said, and glared directly at me.

Most everyone looked at me.

"So now *the rest of us* have to work even harder," Rita said, giving me the evil eye, "to make up for what *one of us* did."

Jeez, what did I do?

"So I want everybody to get out on the sales floor and hustle up those charity donations. We can still win this contest. It will be tough now—really tough, thanks to *one of us*," Rita said. "Not to mention those poor, underprivileged kids who won't get much for Christmas this year, because of *one of us.*"

The other employees glared at me.

"I didn't do anything," I told them.

"Yes, you did," someone said. "You found that dead elf."

"And then you told everybody," somebody else said.

I got major stink-eye from everyone.

"So let's make this contest a success," Rita declared. "Okay, everybody, all together. Ho-ho-Holt's for the holidays!"

Everyone—except me—shouted along with her, then filed out the door.

Rita blocked my path, then gestured to the clipboard that hung above the time clock.

"Check the schedule, princess," she told me, then left.

I hate my life.

On the off chance that today I'd been assigned to a department that I merely disliked, rather than one I absolutely detested, I looked at the schedule.

Huh.   I was supposed to report to one of the assistant managers' offices, along with seven other employees.   Okay, that was weird

I walked down the hallway and saw that the office door was closed.   I knew this was the makeshift dressing room for the actresses portraying the store elves, so I figured I was going to be the elf wrangler again today.   A sign that read "Knock First" was taped to the door.   I knocked.

Jeanette opened the door.   I reeled back in horror, but caught myself before I bolted down the hallway.   She was taking this Summer Santa Sale thing *way* too seriously.   Today she had on a brown dress covered with flecks of red and green.

She looked like a giant fruit cake.

"Come in, Haley," Jeanette said.

I stepped inside and she closed the door behind me.

Around us, girls were changing into elf costumes, jockeying for position at the mirrors to apply their makeup and style their hair around the Santa hats.

My friend Sandy was there.   So was that kinda-sorta slow girl Colleen, and—wow, there were a lot of Holt's employees in there. What the heck?

"Most of the elves quit," Jeanette said.

I got a weird feeling.

"So employees are taking their places," she said, and yanked a garment off a rack.   "Put this on."

Oh my God.   It was an elf costume.

"One of the girls will help you with your hair and makeup," Jeanette said.

Oh my God.   She expected me to wear an elf costume?   And a Santa hat?   And walk around in the store where everyone could see me?

"Hurry up," Jeanette said. "The store opens in twelve minutes."

Oh, crap.

***

Of course, the store was packed.

Kids were running through the aisles, moms were chasing them—well, some of them—teenagers prowled the Juniors Department like roving packs of wolves. Lots of people showed up in Santa suits again today.

Everyone, it seemed, loved the Summer Santa Sale—everyone but me, of course.

The elf costume was a killer. Probably, it was comfortable on the actress it had been assigned to. But judging from the way the shorts were riding up, I figured she was a lot shorter than me.

No way would I leave work today without a serious case of hat-hair. The big, pink circles of rouge on my cheeks made me look like one of those creepy marionettes.

The green, pointed-toed shoes made it nearly impossible to walk quickly, which was way annoying because now customers could easily catch up to me, forcing me to actually wait on them.

I didn't know how my life could get any worse.

Then I knew exactly how.

Rita walked up.

I hate her.

"Are you asking for charity donations?" she demanded.

"Of course," I replied, and eased the donation booklet behind my back. I hadn't asked for any. Mostly, I'd been hiding out in the stockroom.

"Are you telling the customers about our Item of the Day?" she asked.

There was an item of the day?

"Are you telling them about the extra discount we're offering for opening a charge account?" she asked.

No way was I doing that.

"Are you using our ho-ho-Holt's-for-the-holidays slogan?" Rita demanded.

Yeah, okay, I was parading around a midrange department store in a ridiculous elf costume, looking like a complete moron for a pathetic eight dollars an hour. I might, at some point, actually ask a customer for a charity donation. I could even tell them about our Item of the Day—whatever that was. And during a rare planetary alignment, I might mention opening a charge account.

But I was not—absolutely not—going to chant that ridiculous slogan. Not even if they paid me a hundred bucks an hour. Not if they threatened to torture me by making me style my hair in a side-pony, or wear a denim jacket with blue nail polish, or carry a non-designer handbag—okay, well, I might crumble if that happened.

Anyway, this was where I'd drawn a line in the sand.

I was about to scream all of this at Rita when she suddenly walked away.

Damn. I hate it when that happens.

I stood there fuming for a couple of minutes. Then I knew what I had to do.

I had to solve this murder—and quick. It was the only way to get the actresses back to work so I wouldn't have to wear this stupid get-up anymore—and, of course, prove to Detective Madison that he was once again wrong about me.

I headed for the Infants Department. I hate that department—I just hate the department, not actual infants—where I'd seen Alyssa Elgin, one of the actresses brave enough to report back to Holt's this morning. She'd helped me with my hair and makeup in the dressing room.

"Hi, Alyssa," I said, walking up.

She was mid-twenties, I figured, a bit shorter than me, a size four, with red hair and blue eyes.

"It's Haley, right?" Alyssa asked.

I didn't remember introducing myself this morning, but I'd been so traumatized at the prospect of wearing this elf costume, who knows what I said.

"It's really brave of you to come back to work today," I said. "You know, after what happened yesterday."

Alyssa nodded. "Makes me wonder about the other girls who didn't show up today. Like maybe they were involved, or something."

She had a good point, and if I hadn't been so worked up over my own circumstances I might have seen it already. Detective Shuman flashed in my mind. I wondered if he knew about today's no-shows.

"Just you and that other actress came back," I said.

"Nikki Taylor," Alyssa said.

"I'm not exactly loving this costume," I said, and—for what seemed like the hundredth time in the last hour—yanked the shorts down where they belonged. "Do you maybe know any other actresses who'd want to work here?"

"We all came from Extra Extra, so you'd have to contact them," Alyssa said. "It's a company that sends actors out to work background on television and movies, and some Internet projects. Whatever production needs bodies."

I'd heard about companies like that. For a fee, they managed hundreds of people, sending them out on shoots all over Southern California on a daily basis. It was a way for aspiring actors to get some experience, network, and make money while they went on auditions, hunted for an agent, and tried to break into Hollywood.

Another elf walked over from the Boys Department. I'd seen her in the dressing room this morning. She was the only other actress who'd come back to work today.

"Hi, Nikki," I said.

She was young—eighteen, nineteen at the most—pretty, blonde, blue-eyed, short, and one bad Thai meal away from a size two.

"Haley's wondering if we know any other actresses who would want to work here," Alyssa said. "She's not crazy about doing it."

"You are a little tall for an elf," Nikki said with a smile.

Nikki seemed kind of slow. Not I'm-always-a-little-behind-everybody-else slow, more like I've-never-had-to-do-much slow.

"Hey, you know who would definitely want the work?" she said. "Jasmine Grady. She's totally desperate for money."

"Jasmine is an actress?" I asked.

"She's totally committed to making it in this business," Nikki said. She turned to Alyssa. "I'll text her. She's even more desperate for money than the rest of us. If she doesn't find a roommate quick, she's losing her apartment."

"Don't bother," Alyssa said. "She was supposed to work here, but she didn't show up."

"Did she get something else?" Nikki asked, and her eyes lit up. "Maybe *True Blood*? She'd love to work on *True Blood*."

"More like she found out McKenna was working here," Alyssa pointed out.

"Oh …yeah," Nikki said.

My senses jumped to high alert. I'd intended to work the conversation around to the murder of McKenna Crane, but luckily Alyssa beat me to it.

"McKenna and Jasmine were friends?" I asked.

"Used to be roommates," Alyssa said. "Something major happened between them. Jasmine unfriended her on Facebook."

Oh my God. That was major, all right.

"How would Jasmine have found out McKenna was working here?" Nikki asked.

"Maybe she was here," Alyssa said. Her brows shot up in an I'm-just-saying arch. "Maybe she got here early and nobody saw her. She always likes to be early. Then maybe she left ... you know, *early.*"

Nikki gasped. "Oh my God. Are you saying Jasmine might have murdered McKenna?"

I gasped, too. Had I just learned the identity of the murderer? Could it be that easy?

I could stand for something to be easy in my life.

"I'm not saying anything like that," Alyssa insisted. "I'm just thinking that, well, maybe it's possible."

I was with Alyssa on this one. Nobody in the store knew any of the actresses, and after they were in their costumes, they all looked kind of alike. Nobody was watching them. McKenna and Jasmine could have gone into the stockroom together completely unnoticed. They could have argued over something. The whole thing could have gotten out of control and nobody would have known.

Then I remembered the back door in the stockroom. It had been open when I found McKenna's body stuffed in the giant toy bag. At the time I thought it was because the janitor was taking the trash out to the Dumpster. Now it seemed more sinister. Maybe it was Jasmine's escape route after she killed McKenna.

Holt's had security cameras outside the building. I knew from experience—long story—that the cameras in the back covered the loading dock and a small section of the parking lot. But that was it. Somebody could have slipped out the door and not been seen.

Still, this was a great lead.

"Could I get Jasmine's number?" I asked. "I know somebody who's looking for a roommate, too."

Yeah, okay, it was a total lie, but I had to talk to Jasmine.

"That would be great," Nikki said.

We both pulled out our cell phones and she gave me the info.

This was way cool. I'd only been investigating the case for a few minutes and already I had a suspect. I'd go see Jasmine right after my shift ended.

My spirits fell.

No, wait. I couldn't see Jasmine.

I had to go see someone much more deadly than a murder suspect.

My mom.

Chapter 5

My folks still lived in the house I grew up in, a small mansion in La Cañada Flintridge, a town set in the San Gabriel Mountains near Pasadena that overlooked the Los Angeles basin. The house had been left to my mom by her grandmother along with a trust fund. No one knew—or was willing to say—exactly how my great-grandmother had come into such wealth. I thought the bigger mystery was why she'd left it all to my mom, of all people.

Mom was a former beauty queen. Really. She'd worn the crown of Miss California and had placed third in the Miss America pageant before she'd married my dad.

Mom still thought she was a beauty queen.

My dad was an aerospace engineer doing top secret work for the government which gave him, luckily, lots of excuses to be gone from the house for days on end, and unable to tell anyone where he'd been.

Not that my mom noticed.

I had an older brother who was an Air Force pilot flying F-16s in the Middle East, and a younger sister who attended UCLA and did some modeling.

When I was a child, Mom had devoted herself to turning me into a show pony—I mean a pageant queen—like herself. She'd subjected me to every type of lesson imaginable—singing, piano, tap, ballet, modeling—in an all-out effort to discover in me some tiny nugget of actual talent. She'd finally given up when, at age nine, I set fire to the den curtains twirling fire batons—which was a total accident. Really. I swear.

Anyway, my younger sister had turned out to be a Mom-clone and had filled her stilettos to perfection, much to everyone's relief.

As I parked in the circular driveway outside my folks' house, I decided I should give Detective Shuman a call—strictly in the line of duty, of course. Never mind that he was kind of hot. I had a civic obligation to assist law enforcement in a murder investigation.

That's just the kind of model citizen I am.

I wasn't sure if Shuman knew about all the elf actresses who'd not reported back for work at Holt's today. It seemed to me this was a vital clue he should be aware of. I mean, if I'd murdered someone and stuffed her body into a giant toy bag, I wouldn't have come back to work.

I pulled out my cell and placed the call. While the phone rang, I wondered if I should mention what Alyssa and Nikki had told me about Jasmine Grady, how she and McKenna had been roommates before something happened to end their friendship.

I didn't like the idea of throwing Jasmine out there—although Alyssa hadn't seemed to mind one bit. I wanted to talk to her first. It sounded as if her life was tough enough already, without being interviewed by homicide detectives.

But I didn't get to tell Shuman anything. My call went to voicemail. I left a message asking him to call me and hung up.

For a couple more minutes I sat in the car looking at my parents' house. I knew I had to go inside and talk to Mom. Jack had asked for my help. Brooke was depending on me. It was the right thing to do.

I hate it when I have to do the right thing.

Juanita, the housekeeper who'd worked for my folks as long as I could remember, met me at the door. We chatted for a couple of minutes. She asked how my life was going and I asked about her two grown daughters. Finally, there was nothing left to do but talk to Mom.

"She's in the den," Juanita said.

Because Mom seems to think the next step she took might be down a runway, or that the paparazzi was waiting on the front lawn to take her picture and post it on the giant screen in Times Square, she always dressed to impress—even if it was only to impress herself.

I found her in the den, stretched out on a chaise, reading *Vogue* and holding a glass of wine. She wore a Vera Wang dress, three inch heels, and a full complement of jewelry. Her dark hair was styled to perfection and held in place with enough spray to withstand a category five hurricane.

Just your average housewife, passing the time on a summer afternoon.

That was my mom.

"Oh," she huffed, slapping at a page in the magazine. "You won't *believe* what the designers are attempting to do to us this fall."

I saw no need to respond.

"It's a travesty," Mom declared.

There was nothing I could say to that.

She sipped her wine. "I don't know what they're thinking."

Note: Mom didn't ask me about my life but her housekeeper did.

She got quiet for a moment. She stared across the room, focusing on nothing.

"Maybe I should start my own fashion line," she said.

Mom's idea of running a business wasn't like everyone else's. Her usual process for most any new project was to come up with some wild notion, pour an unseemly amount of money into it, then turn it over to someone else to run.

Of course, occasionally Mom came up with a winner. Not long ago she'd started a fruit arrangement business that had been the hit of Los Angeles, right up to the point where somebody was poisoned and somebody else was murdered—long story. No way could I go through that again.

I jumped in.

"You know, Mom, no matter what the designers are showing, it will look great on you," I said.

She thought about it for a few seconds. "I suppose you're right. But—"

"Ty and I want to go to the charity event at the Staffords' this year," I said, cutting her off and hoping to divert her attention from further thoughts of herself.

Okay, that was a total lie. Ty didn't even know about the Staffords' party, or if he did, he hadn't mentioned it to me. But he'd be okay with going. His family had been perched high atop the L.A. social ladder for generations and routinely involved itself with this sort of event.

"You do? That would be lovely," Mom said.

Right away, I saw her thoughts turn like a laser-guided bomb to my relationship with Ty. He was handsome, wealthy, and successful, which made him among the most highly-coveted bachelors. I knew she was thinking *wedding*.

"How is Ty?" she asked.

"He's great," I said.

Okay, that was sort-of a lie. I had no idea if he was great or not, since I hadn't heard from him in a while.

I knew I had to change the subject again before Mom started making suggestions for my head piece and bouquet.

"Do you have a dress for the Staffords' party?" I asked. "I'd love to see it."

"Oh, well, of course."

Mom set her wine glass aside and rose from the chaise. I followed her upstairs as she blabbed on about something. I, of course, ignored her with practiced ease, a skill I'd learned at a very young age which had served me well at every job I'd had, every class I'd taken, and every meeting I'd attended.

The house had been built back in the twenties or thirties, maybe. It had high ceilings and expansive spaces, statuary niches, dark wood and hand-carved crown moldings. A few years ago, Mom had knocked out some of the walls in the back of the house and created a huge master suite. It had four walk-in closets—one for each season—and another tiny one that my dad was allowed to use.

Mom had consulted with a decorator for weeks—eventually driving the old gal to abandon her chosen profession and go to work as a Wal-mart greeter—and had finally decided on a color scheme of beige and white. One of Mom's talents—or gifts, as she likes to call them—was recognizing the subtle differences between ecru, beige, eggshell, cream, tan, linen, and taupe, and neon white, snow white, bright white, winter white, alabaster, ivory, and just plain white.

I'm pretty sure that's on her résumé.

"I don't know whether I should wear the gold Halston, or the red YSL," Mom said, throwing open the doors of one of her closets.

I settled into a chair—I'm pretty sure it was alabaster—near the patio doors that overlooked the flower garden.

"Red for this time of year?" I asked. "Are you going patriotic?"

Mom froze. She turned to me with an on-my-god look on her face.

I get that a lot.

"The event is a fundraiser for Christmas," she told me. "The theme for the evening is Christmas. Everyone will be dressed in Christmas attire. Black tie. Had you forgotten that?"

Yes, believe it or not, I had.

This seemed like an excellent time to change the subject.

"I met an actress the other day," I said.

Luckily, Mom had gotten distracted by the gowns in her closet and didn't ask any questions about how or where. I'd never actually gotten around to telling her that I worked for Holt's. I never got around to telling my mom a lot of things.

I'm not even sure she knew where I lived.

"So I was wondering," I said. "Did you ever want to be an actress?"

Mom came out of the closet with a silver beaded Gucci gown.

"Acting? Oh, no, never," she said. She held the dress up, tilted her head left, then right. "It's very demeaning. Living hand to mouth, barely making ends meet, borrowing money from friends and family. Actors spend most of their time looking for work, trying to get an agent."

"The actress I met was working as an extra," I said.

"Even worse," Mom said. "Background people are herded around like cattle, yelled at, talked down to. They're underpaid, sometimes."

"It doesn't sound very glamorous," I said.

Mom held the gown in front of her and studied her reflection in the mirror. "And, of course, there's the issue of the casting couch," she said.

No way was I talking about sex with my mom.

I sprang out of my chair.

"I've got to get to class," I said.

Mom knew I attended college—although I'm not sure she knew which one—but she didn't know I wasn't taking any classes during the summer quarter, allowing me to use my all-time favorite excuse to leave most any place, at most any time.

"I'll add Ty and me to the Staffords' guest list on my way out," I said, heading for the door.

Mom said something but I didn't hang around long enough to listen.

I went downstairs to the room at the back of the house that Mom used for an office. It was decorated in browns and deep reds, with just a touch of pewter. A big mahogany desk sat in the middle of the room, surrounded by pictures of herself.

I pulled up a chair and logged on to Mom's computer. I'd figured out her password long ago—her own name—so I had no trouble accessing the file containing the guest list for the charity event at the Stafford house.

Nobody got into one of these things without an invitation, and nobody got an invitation unless they were *somebody*, or knew *somebody*. Putting Ty and me on the list wouldn't raise an eyebrow, but adding Jack's name would create two different problems.

First, if I used his real name and something went sideways while he was searching the house for little Hope, everything could be traced back to not only Jack and Brooke, but also the Pike Warner law firm.

Second, if I used his real name nobody would know who he was, somebody would question why he'd been invited, and everything might hit the fan after all.

I knew how to get around both of those problems.

I pulled up Mom's email and scrolled through her inbox until I found messages referencing the guest list. Just as I'd expected, Mom was being Mom. The other members of the committee had sent her the names of those people who would attend. Mom had just cut and pasted them onto the list.

That's my mom's idea of heading up a committee.

I clicked on the file containing the guest list. On the drive over here I'd come up with a new identity for Jack, one that would let him walk through the Staffords' front door with ease, though I still thought rappelling onto the roof from a helicopter would be more fun.

I entered his name on the list as "Jackson Blair."

I pulled up Mom's email again and dashed off a quick message announcing to the other committee members that Jackson Blair, entrepreneur and philanthropist, and owner of Blair Group International in South Africa, had graciously accepted her invitation to attend blah, blah, blah. I signed Mom's name and hit "send."

Yeah, okay, this was a little risky but I felt like I had it covered.

If someone mentioned it to Mom—and I knew someone was bound to do just that—I was sure she'd roll with it. The list had over one hundred names on it and she couldn't possibly know every one of them. Plus, she wouldn't want to admit she didn't know Jackson Blair if everyone else did.

Occasionally, Mom's vanity came in handy.

With the party just days away, I doubted Ty would be back from New York in time to attend.

Of course, if he'd ever call me, I'd know.

But no way was I staying home—not with Jack there. I wasn't missing out on a totally cool clandestine investigation with a totally hot private detective—oh, and I wanted to get Brooke's daughter back for her, of course.

I added Ty's name and my name to the guest list, then logged off of Mom's computer and left the house.

Everything was in place, everything had been done.

All I needed to do now was find a fabulous gown to wear—and an awesome handbag, of course. The Breathless wasn't right for this occasion, but I knew there was a purse out there somewhere that was.

I headed for the mall.

Chapter 6

Leaving Mom's house, I called my best friend Marcie and asked her to go shopping with me. She couldn't make it because of a family thing. It was a major disappointment, but we decided to get together later. She promised to bring this month's *Cosmo*. It was their Quiz Blow-Out issue, and we absolutely had to find out where our lives ranked on important matters such as flip-flops, up-dos, little black dresses, finding a boyfriend, keeping a boyfriend, and, of course, dumping a boyfriend.

I was tempted to hit the mall on my own. I hadn't bought a new purse in a while and the Breathless was burning in my brain like a star atop a Christmas tree, but I fought it off.

I can be strong like that when I have to.

Instead, I phoned Jasmine. I told her Nikki had given me her number, and gave her the whole my-friend-needs-a-roommate story. She said to come over. I hit the Starbucks drive-thru and got a mocha frappuccino—my favorite drink in the entire world—then headed out the 210 toward Canyon Country.

I hung a right off of Soledad Canyon Road onto Camp Plenty Drive and parked at the curb outside her apartment building. You could tell the complex had been there for thirty years, or something. The buildings were stucco with red tile roofs, the trim painted an I-love-the-80's green.

I left my car and followed the sidewalk back into the complex, then hoofed it up some steep concrete stairs to the second floor. The place looked clean enough and the area seemed safe.

Jasmine answered the door. I expected her to look pretty much like the other elf actresses, and she did—mid-twenties, brown hair, brown eyes, able to squeeze into size two blue jeans without holding in her stomach.

"Yeah, great, come in," she said, after I introduced myself.

I stepped into her living room. A little kitchen was off to the left, and I saw a hallway that I figured led to the bathroom and bedrooms. Vertical blinds covered the windows and the slider that led to a balcony.

The place was small and furnished with a couch covered with a worn-looking quilt, TV tables for end tables, a television sitting on a wooden crate, and a beanbag chair with duct tape running up the side and across the top. A laptop was set up on a card table. There were lots of framed photographs and a few decorator items. Everything was probably discount store or flea market finds, but I figured it was the best she could afford. Still, the place looked cold and empty.

I guess she really wanted to become an actress if she was okay with living like this.

I mean that in the nicest way, of course.

"Want something to drink?" Jasmine asked, heading for the kitchen. "I've got some soda."

"Just water," I called. "I've had too many sodas today already."

That wasn't true, of course, but I felt guilty drinking anything that cost her actual money.

I ambled over to the card table and looked at the framed photographs surrounding the laptop. They were mostly shots of Jasmine and her friends, laughing, mugging for the camera, wearing shorts outside Grauman's Chinese Theater, super short dresses outside a club, and bathing suits at the beach, each outfit fully accessorized, of course. My gaze jumped to their handbags—old habit—and I noted a Dooney & Bourke barrel, a Prada hobo, a Gucci tote and a Burberry satchel—all knock-offs.

I spotted another photo on the floor half buried under a stack of Jasmine's headshots. I picked it up.

It was a picture of McKenna. I'd only seen her that one time, dead, stuffed inside the giant toy bag, but I recognized her. In the photo she was at a party at someone's house, dancing. Her dress was hiked up a little, her arms were in the air, her long red hair was swinging. She was alone on the dance floor. In the background, a crowd of people were holding drinks, talking, laughing. I didn't recognize any of them.

Sensing Jasmine behind me, I turned and held up the photo.

"I guess you heard about McKenna," I said.

She passed me a glass of water. "It's all over Facebook."

"You two used to be friends?" I asked, even though I already knew.

"Roommates," Jasmine said. "McKenna didn't have a lot of friends."

I laid the picture aside. "She looks popular here," I said.

"She was popular until you got to know her," she said, then nodded toward the hallway. "You want to see the bedroom?"

The tour didn't take two minutes. Jasmine pointed out the shared bathroom. The bedroom she wanted to rent out contained a mattress set on a frame and a chest of drawers somebody had painted purple and covered with 'N Sync stickers.

I caught a glimpse of Jasmine's bedroom next door. A mattress lay on the floor. Her clothes were stacked on a couple of TV trays.

These weren't exactly five-star accommodations, but everything was clean, and I guess if you were desperate—which I figured most actresses were—this was at least a roof over your head.

"So this friend of yours," Jasmine said, leading the way back to the living room. "She's got a job, right? She'll pay her half on time?"

"Sure. No problem," I said. "She had a couple of questions."

Jasmine plopped down on the couch and curled her legs beneath her.

"I don't care what she does as long as she pays me on the first," she told me.

Okay, now I was feeling kind of bad for pretending I knew someone who wanted to rent the room. But what could I do except roll with it?

"How come McKenna moved out?" I asked, as I sat down on the other end of the couch and put my glass on the card table. "Does the apartment have, you know, unwanted roommates like bugs or something?"

"McKenna was always late with her rent money. She got way behind. I had to make up the difference because it's my name on the lease," Jasmine said. "Then she skipped out on me."

"She didn't pay you? Not at all?"

"Bitch," Jasmine muttered.

She pulled her cell phone from her pocket and began fiddling with it.

"Do you think McKenna's family might make it right?" I asked, trying to bring her back to our conversation.

"I doubt it," she said, glancing up from the phone. She shook her head. "And I was close—so close—to getting the cash from McKenna."

"She got a job?" I asked.

"She got struck by lightning," Jasmine said, turning back to her phone. "A role in a sitcom. Prime time. A major network. Starting at twenty grand an episode."

"Twenty thousand dollars? Every week?" I might have yelled that.

"Don't ask me how, but she got it," Jasmine said.

"So what the heck was she doing working as an elf at Holt's?" I asked.

I mean, jeez, if I had a job pulling down twenty big ones a week I wouldn't even drive past a Holt's store, let alone go inside.

"Production hadn't started yet.   She needed money.   But mostly, I think she liked being around the rest of us so she could brag," Jasmine said.   She turned back to her phone, then said, "Hang on a second. I have to submit for this audition."

I leaned forward a bit to try and see what she was doing, and asked, "You can get an audition on the Internet?"

"If you don't have an agent," Jasmine said, working her phone.

"Like Extra Extra?" I asked.

"Not exactly," she said. "A lot of productions will take actors who aren't in the Screen Actors Guild yet.   They post casting notices. I signed up for this service so I can submit my headshot and acting résumé directly to the casting director, and try to get an audition."

"Did McKenna do that, too?" I asked.

Jasmine huffed and said, "Look, McKenna was a bitch.   She treated me like trash.   She treated everybody like trash.   She skipped out on me and moved in with this guy who had the serious hots for her—not because she cared about him.   She didn't.   She just used him because she needed a place to live."

I didn't know what to say to that, which was just as well since Jasmine kept talking.

"And when she got her big break, that sitcom role, she became an even bigger bitch," Jasmine said.   "Throwing it in everybody's face about how she was going to hire a personal assistant, buy a condo on the beach, vacation in Europe, start doing movies.   She went on and on about what she'd wear to all the award shows, about how great her life was—when the rest of us are lucky if we eat three times a day."

Jasmine looked angry—and I can't say that I blamed her.   Still, what better time to push her for a little more info?

"So if you needed money so bad, why did you cancel on the elf thing at Holt's?" I asked.

Jasmine fumed, bouncing her fist off her thigh, staring off at nothing like she was remembering every bad thing McKenna had ever done to her.

"Did you come to the store that morning at all?" I asked.

A few more seconds passed, then Jasmine sat back on the couch.

"I'm sorry. I shouldn't have gone off like that about McKenna," she said. "It's just that I want this so bad. I want to act. It's like some crazy passion that I can't control. Did you ever feel that way about something?"

Did designer handbags count?

"And my mom." Jasmine's emotions spun up again. "She's ragging me big-time to give up on trying to make it as an actress and move back home. To Scottsdale."

"Ugh," I said. Scottsdale was probably a really nice place, but not if your dream was to become an actress.

"Yeah. And she keeps talking to me about this guy I went to high school with who's going to inherit his dad's Kia dealership in like fifty years, or something, like that's going to lure me back home."

"Oh my God," I said.

"Look at this."

Jasmine launched off the couch, and pulled a gift box from under a stack of magazines on the floor beside the TV.

I recognized the logo. My heart began to beat faster.

She ripped open the box and thrust a Coach wristlet at me. I took it, cradled it in my palms, giving it the tender, loving care it deserved. I caressed its supple leather, breathed in the rich aroma.

There's nothing like the smell of a new handbag.

"Mom sent me this thing with a note telling me that I could have nice stuff like this all the time, if I came home and married boring-to-the-bone Kia guy," she said, throwing the box into the floor. "It's a Coach—"

"—laser cut Op Art large wristlet from their Madison line, with perforated leather in an eyelet lace pattern, an inside open pocket, zip-top closure, fabric lining, available in silver and parchment, that retails for two hundred bucks," I said.

Jeez, maybe I should get a life.

"I don't *need* a two-hundred dollar wristlet," Jasmine said. "What I *need* is grocery money."

"Why don't you—"

My throat went dry. I couldn't say the words, yet I had to.

I gulped hard and tried again.

"Why don't you ... return it?" I asked.

"She didn't include the receipt. I took it to their store at the Northridge Mall—where I was treated like Julia Roberts on Rodeo Drive *before* Richard Gere shopped with her, by the way," Jasmine said. "They would only give me store credit."

"I'll buy it from you."

The words popped out of my mouth before I could stop them—not that I wanted to.

Jasmine just looked at me for a couple of minutes, like she was wondering if she'd heard me right, if I really meant it, what I did to earn that much money, or maybe who I was sleeping with who gave me that kind of cash.

I saw no reason to get into it with her.

I grabbed my purse and pulled out the two one-hundred dollar bills I kept hidden in my cosmetic bag. It was my don't-get-embarrassed-at-checkout-if-my-credit-card-is-declined emergency fund.

Yeah, okay, this was, technically, Jasmine's emergency, not mine. But I felt really bad for her and I wanted to do something to help. Plus, the Coach wristlet was awesome.

I held out the money.

Jasmine didn't jump at it. She just stared, then said, "Are you serious?"

"I never kid about designer handbags," I told her.

"Oh, wow." She collapsed onto the couch again and covered her face with her palms. She sniffed.

Oh my God, was she crying?

I'm not good with a crier.

Jasmine sniffed again, dug her fists into her eyes, then looked up at me. Her eyes were red but—whew!—she wasn't shedding tears.

"It's just that, well, nobody's ever done something like this for me before," she said softly.

"It's a great wristlet. I'm thrilled to have it," I said.

I put the money on the couch, then grabbed the box off of the floor and put the wristlet inside.

"Thank you," Jasmine said, gazing up at me. "Thanks so much."

I could tell she really meant it. But I'm not big on emotional scenes, so I headed for the door.

"Let me know about your friend," Jasmine said, following me.

It took me a second to realize she was talking about my imaginary friend whom I'd said wanted to share the apartment.

"Oh, yeah, sure," I said. "I'll let you know."

"Thanks," Jasmine called, as I went down the stairs.

Okay, despite giving her money for the wristlet—which was really as much for me as it was for her—I felt like a jerk. I'd come here using the I-have-a-friend excuse because I'd thought Jasmine might have murdered McKenna. While it sounded as if McKenna hadn't endeared herself to Jasmine—or anyone else—Jasmine didn't have any reason to kill her. In fact, keeping her alive would have benefited her greatly, because she could have gotten her back-rent out of McKenna from the astronomical first paycheck she was going to receive from the sitcom.

I walked to my car.

Now, of course, somehow I was going to have to find Jasmine a roommate. Or maybe I'd just pay half her rent for her. Or maybe I could get Ty to buy a production company and cast her in some big movie.

And why hadn't Ty called me? Where was my official boyfriend when I needed him?

Crap.

I got in my car, cranked up the air conditioning and called Ty—which didn't suit me but there it was. He answered—surprise, surprise—right away.

"I'm really glad you called," Ty said. He sounded tired, a little weary. "I had a day like you wouldn't believe. First thing this morning ..."

His words turned into blah, blah, blah, and I drifted off thinking about McKenna getting her big break landing a role in a sitcom, then getting murdered.

Wow, was that lousy timing, or what?

"Haley?" Ty asked.

I realized he'd finished talking and had probably asked me something.

"Are you there?" he asked, sounding concerned.

Honestly, you'd think that by now he'd be used to me not listening to him.

"I'm here," I said. "Listen, I'd like us to go to the Christmas charity fundraiser this year. It's Saturday night. Will you be back by then?"

I heard some shuffling in the background and imagined Ty checking his calendar.

"I've got a meeting," he said. "I'll try to make it, but I can't guarantee it."

One thing about Ty, he never made a promise he couldn't keep. He maintained a record of 100% reliability on this issue by simply never promising anything.

"I'll text you the info, just in case," I said.

He was quiet for a few seconds—I thought maybe he'd gotten distracted by the allure of a new spreadsheet—then said, "I miss you, Haley."

That was nice to hear. It made my stomach feel warm and kind of gooey.

But before I could tell him that I missed him, too, he said, "I've got to run. I'll talk to you again soon."

He hung up before I could say goodbye.

Okay, that wasn't exactly the official boyfriend-girlfriend I-can't-live-without-you-conversation I'd hoped for.

I decided my day needed a boost.

The Coach wristlet I'd bought from Jasmine seemed kind of sad, just sitting there in the box on the seat next to me. I decided a new Breathless handbag to put it in would make us both feel better.

Just as I was about to pull away from the curb, I caught sight of Jasmine in a faded Saturn driving out of her apartment complex. I was going to wave, but she didn't see me.

I wondered if she was headed for the grocery store to stock up using the money I'd just paid her, while here I sat with visions of a new handbag dancing in my head.

Not a great feeling.

No way could I go shopping now.

I admired the fact that she was willing to live the way she lived because she was so devoted to her acting. From what my mom had told me, actors attempting to break into the business weren't treated all that well on-set. They had financial problems, and Jasmine sure seemed to have more than her share of those. Plus, she had to deal with her mom tempting her with expensive gifts, and trying to marry her off to that guy from high school with the maybe-one-day Kia dealership.

It was a hard life. It almost sounded like it could be a Lifetime movie.

A jolt hit my brain—and I hadn't even had any chocolate recently.

Sitting upstairs and listening to Jasmine talk, I'd believed everything she said. In fact, I'd gotten so caught up in her story I'd bought that Coach wristlet.

Now I realized she'd never answered my questions about why, if she was so desperate for money, she'd cancelled on the elf job at Holt's. I'd asked her if she'd come to the store at all that morning, and she hadn't responded. Instead, she'd launched into that story about her mom.

Had she just gotten so wrapped up in her own problems that she'd forgotten I'd asked her those things?

Or had she used those problems to distract me?

I thought about it for a minute. Jasmine had seemed genuinely upset and distraught about her mom, the Kia guy, McKenna skipping out, and trying to make rent.

But maybe she'd fooled me.

She was, after all, an actress.

Chapter 7

Six minutes to go.

I sat in my car outside Holt's the next morning, enjoying my last few minutes of freedom—and the mocha frappuccino I'd picked up from Starbucks—before I had to clock-in. The parking lot was filling up with employees arriving for work. The janitor was in front of the store cleaning the big glass windows.

Nobody looked happy.

Since I was forced to wear that elf costume, I was also forced to show up a half hour early so I'd have time to squeeze into the thing, do my makeup, and put on that oh-so attractive Santa hat. Luckily, my apartment was near the store. It only took seven minutes to drive here—six, if I ran the light at the corner—but somehow I'd ended up arriving a few minutes earlier than required.

Obviously, I was going to have to be more diligent about adhering to my established morning routine so this never happened again.

I'd awakened thinking about Christmas—thanks to that hideous elf costume, no doubt—and immediately it hit me that now would be a good time to get a jump on my holiday shopping.

Really, it's never too early to think about shopping.

Since I had six minutes to kill, I pulled the list that I'd started this morning over my bowl of Coco Puffs from my bag—an awesome Prada tote—and looked it over.

My BFF Marcie topped my list, of course, as a BFF should. I considered giving her the Coach wristlet I'd bought from Jasmine last night, along with a Coach handbag. I'd love to have it myself, so I knew she would, too.

Next on the list was my sister. She'd die for a L.A.M.B. tote— who wouldn't? I'd penciled Mom in for a Ralph Lauren satchel.

Wow, do I have great gift ideas for friends and family, or what?

Then it hit me. I should make my own wish list.

I flipped the paper over, dug a pen from my tote, and wrote my name at the top of the page.

One of the most annoying things about any gift-giving occasion was when the gift recipient insisted they didn't know what they wanted, they couldn't think of anything they needed, blah, blah, blah. I mean, really, how could you *not* know of something you'd like to have?   At any given moment, I could recite ten things I wanted, right off the top of my head.

Immediately, I jotted down a DKNY crossbody and a Lucky Brand satchel, and since you can never have too many satchels, I added the Ralph Lauren bag I'd thought I'd get for Mom. The image of a Louis Vuitton tote sprang into my head—I get that a lot—so I added it to my list. And what gift-giving occasion would be complete without a clutch bag? A Gucci would do quite nicely, I decided, and wrote that down.

All of these required matching wallets, of course, so I noted that, too.

My heart began to beat a little faster just looking at the list.

Images of Christmas flashed in my mind. Me, surrounded by beautifully wrapped gifts. Me, cutting the ribbons, tearing off wrapping paper, ripping open boxes, tossing aside mounds of tissue paper to discover one gorgeous handbag after another.

Hang on a minute.

What if I gave my wish list to my friends and family, and somehow, all of them ended up giving me the exact same purse? Oh my God, that would be awful.

There was only way to prevent this Christmas nightmare from happening.

I was going to have to assign gifts this year.

I glanced at my watch and saw that two minutes remained before I had to clock-in, the exact amount of time necessary to walk into the store at a moderate pace, reach the break room, store my handbag in my locker, and get in line at the time clock with fifteen seconds or less to spare.

Since Holt's didn't pay employees for standing in line, I saw no reason to get there early.

Still, I didn't like to be late for work.   Holt's employee attendance policy stated that if you were late for work the cashiers' supervisor wrote your name on the whiteboard in the break room. This meant a confrontation with Rita—I hate her—and while I actually enjoyed a good confrontation, dealing with Rita—I hate her—isn't the best way to begin a four-hour stretch in a place I really didn't want to be.

Plus, if you got your name on the board four times in one month, you got fired. I wasn't all that excited about keeping this job, but I wasn't about to give Rita—I hate her—the satisfaction of dropping the ax on me.

I put my wish list and pen in my tote and got out of my car. Just as I hit the button to lock the doors, a car zoomed into the space next to me. Detective Shuman got out.

My heart did its usual little oh-wow flip-flop whenever I saw Shuman—which was bad of me, I know, but there it was.

Then my heart did an oh-no flip-flop when I realized that Detective Madison might be with him. No way did I want to start off my day dealing with him.

But then I saw that Shuman was alone. My heart did an oh-whew flip-flop as I walked to the back of my car to meet him.

Shuman looked pretty good this morning. He had on a brown sport coat with khaki trousers and a yellow shirt. He'd paired these with a teal tie, for no apparent reason. Jeez, where was his girlfriend? Wasn't she dressing him?

My heart did a little I'm-glad-and-I-shouldn't-be flip-flop when I realized this probably meant the two of them weren't living together yet.

"Solve McKenna's murder?" I asked, giving him a smile.

"Sure did," he said. "Hers and six more just yesterday."

Nothing like a little homicide humor first thing in the morning.

"You called me yesterday," Shuman said.

I figured he'd call me back sometime today when he had time. This was way better—I mean that strictly as a concerned citizen anxious to aid law enforcement, of course.

"I didn't know if you'd gotten word that only two of the elves reported back to work after the murder," I said. "Made me wonder about why the others didn't show up. Most of them were scared, I guess. But maybe one of them was involved in McKenna's death somehow."

Shuman pulled a little tablet from the inside pocket of his jacket. "Who are they?"

I gave him Alyssa and Nikki's names.

Like most homicide detectives, Shuman was tight-lipped about an ongoing murder investigation. But we'd worked together on a few cases in the past—and I am, after all, *me*—so he was a little freer with details.

"The victim was struck on the head with a nutcracker," Shuman said.

"The big wooden ones that look kind of like soldiers?" I asked.

I remembered seeing dozens of them tangled with the other Christmas decorations on the floor of the stockroom the morning I'd found McKenna. The image of her being struck on the head with one of those things flashed in my head. I pushed it away.

"Fingerprints?" I asked.

"Lots of prints," he said. "Nothing yet that's any help."

"Motive?" I asked.

He gave me cop-face—which was way hot, of course—so I knew he wasn't going to give up anything else, unless I had something to offer.

"McKenna had just gotten a role in a sitcom," I said. "Starting at—get this—twenty grand an episode."

Shuman's brows rose, and I was pretty sure I could see his thoughts spinning out a motive. "Professional jealousy?"

"TV roles don't have understudies. The production company would just re-cast the part, and there's no guarantee who they'd pick," I said.

"That's a lot of money up for grabs," Shuman said.

Greed was a favorite motive among homicide detectives and murderers alike, and following the money trail usually paid off. I couldn't disagree that somebody—especially a starving actress—would kill for it. Still, I thought there was something else going on.

"McKenna wasn't well liked even before she got the role," I said.

Yesterday when I'd left Jasmine's apartment, I'd wondered if she was just playing me by using her acting skills to avoid answering my questions, and instead make me feel sorry for her. Maybe she was honest and sincere. I couldn't tell for sure. Either way, I couldn't hold back with Shuman.

"Talk to Jasmine Grady," I said. "She and McKenna were roommates. McKenna skipped out on her owing back-rent. It really left Jasmine in a jam."

Shuman jotted down the name.

"Did you know McKenna was living with her boyfriend?" I asked.

"Trent Daniels," Shuman said. "I talked to him yesterday."

"McKenna moved in with him after she left Jasmine's place," I said. "According to Jasmine, the guy was crazy about her. She just wanted free rent."

"If McKenna was using him, he didn't know it," Shuman said. "Or maybe he didn't care."

Or maybe Jasmine had made the whole thing up to throw suspicion off of herself.

"Do you think he really loved her?" I asked.

"I think he was a little weird. I've still got to run a background check on him," Shuman said. He tapped his tablet. "Money troubles are usually the best leads."

We stood there for a couple of minutes, quiet, both of us lost in thought, then Shuman said, "I'd better go."

Activity in the parking lot had ceased. No more I'm-desperate-for-a-job employees pulled up, parked, and went inside. That could only mean I was late for my shift.

"Me, too," I said.

Still, we just stood there looking at each other until wo both realized what we were doing.

"See you," Shuman said, walking away.

"Yeah, okay," I said, and headed for the store.

At the door I stopped and looked back. Shuman stood outside of his car watching me.

My heart did another flip-flop, and I went inside.

Already, the Christmas trees on display were lit. "Frosty the Snowman" played on the store's public address system. The giant toy bag sat at the ready near the fake fireplace.

I hurried back to the break room. No one was inside, not even Rita—I hate her. I thought that maybe I'd gotten lucky and she was late for work, too, but then I saw my name already written on the whiteboard.

Damn.

Yeah, okay, I was late for work because I'd been talking to Shuman in the parking lot, but that was way better than talking to him here in the store. I'd die—absolutely die—if Shuman or anyone else I knew caught me wearing that elf costume.

I've really got to get a handle on my life.

I clocked-in, stowed my tote—after I erased my name from the whiteboard, of course—and went to the elf dressing room down the hall. Mostly Holt's employees were inside. The only actresses present were Alyssa and Nikki. My spirits dipped a little. None of the other actresses had come back.

Everyone seemed to be in a good mood, talking and laughing, taking turns getting into their costumes behind the privacy curtain. Others applied makeup and styled their hair in front of the mirrors.

"Hi, Haley," Alyssa said. "How's it going?"

"I'm still not loving the costume," I said, grabbing it off the rack. "Can't you get any of your actress friends to come back to work?"

"Not likely." She leaned toward the mirror and applied bright red lipstick. "Not with that homicide detective outside the store."

I caught her gaze in the mirror.

"You mean Detective Shuman?" I asked.

I guess I shouldn't have been surprised that Alyssa remembered Shuman from the day of McKenna's murder and recognized him this morning. First of all, Shuman was kind of hot. Second, Alyssa had probably never dealt much with a homicide detective. Both were good reasons for Shuman to stick in her head.

"Does he have any idea who killed McKenna?" Alyssa asked.

Immediately, I felt like I was a homicide detective myself— which was way cool, of course—and reluctant to divulge info about the investigation.

"He's following a number of leads," I said.

"Did he talk to Jasmine Grady?" she asked, turning to me. "She was majorly mad when McKenna ditched her owing back-rent."

"I'm not sure," I said.

"He really needs to talk to Trent," Alyssa said. "Tell that detective to talk to Trent. Trent Daniels. He was totally in love with her, and she treated him like garbage."

"Yeah, I'll do that," I said.

I went behind the privacy curtain and changed into the elf costume. When I came out, most of the girls were gone. Alyssa was still in front of the mirror.

"Listen, Haley," she said. "Maybe I should talk to that detective myself, tell him everything about McKenna. She was a real bitch to just about everybody."

Alyssa seemed concerned about finding McKenna's killer. But I guess that was normal since she really needed to work and was probably a little afraid that some psycho elf murderer was on the loose in the store and she might be the next victim.

Still, like with Jasmine, I couldn't be sure whether she was genuinely concerned or if something else was going on. Who knew with actresses?

"I heard that McKenna had just gotten a role in a sitcom," I said. "Did you know that?"

"Everybody knew it." Alyssa turned back to the mirror. "McKenna made sure of it."

"How did that happen?" I asked.

"I have no idea," Alyssa said.

"She never said?" I asked. "Wasn't she blabbing about it to everyone?"

"Well, she didn't tell me," Alyssa said. "I'd better get out there."

She grabbed her handbag off the floor to store in her assigned locker in the break room, and my heart did a totally unexpected oh-wow flutter. Alyssa had a Louis Vuitton satchel. It was gorgeous. I definitely needed to add that to my Christmas wish list.

Jeez, how could Alyssa—a struggling actress—afford such a mega expensive bag? I wondered if maybe her mom was tempting her with pricey handbags to try and convince her to give up on acting and come home, as Jasmine's mother was doing.

Alyssa slung the satchel over her shoulder and disappeared out the door.

My spirits dipped. False alarm.

Alyssa's satchel was a knock-off—and not even a good one. The handles were wrong, which was always a dead giveaway, plus the classic LVT print had been mixed with their checkerboard pattern in a way that screamed I-can't-afford-a-genuine-bag-so-I-bought-this-thing.

I've got an eye for counterfeit handbags. Marcie and I had been buying knock-off designer bags from the Garment District and giving purse parties for a long time now, so I could spot a fake from a mile away.

By the time I'd put on my elf makeup and Santa hat, I was the last one to leave the dressing room. The store was open now and I could hear the usual commotion from shoppers on the sales floor along with strains of "Winter Wonderland" on the PA.

I spotted Jeanette standing in the hallway. Yikes! How many more fashion fiascos should I be expected to endure for minimum wage?

Today she had on a dress—white, with a black collar and, for no conceivable reason, a yellow ruffle at the hem.

She looked like an over-stuffed Christmas goose.

I expected Jeanette to give me the evil eye for being tardy, but she was busy talking to someone.

He was a big guy, well over six feet tall, maybe mid-twenties with dark hair that had needed a trim at least a month ago. He wore jeans and a faded, slightly stretched-out T-shirt with "Brooks & Dunn" and steer horns printed on the front. Somehow, he looked familiar.

I stopped at the customer service booth. My friend Grace was on duty. We'd worked in the booth together lots of times and shared the same ideas on customer service—none of which would be found in the official Holt's handbook.

Grace was about my age and attended college—which, for some reason, she actually liked—and always did the coolest things with her hair. Not long ago she'd dyed it Martian green. Topped today with a Santa hat, the look put a whole new spin on Christmas.

Two customers waited in line but Grace ignored them—see why we get along so well?—and brought me one of the charity donation booklets that management insisted had to be stored there.

"We're not doing so great in the contest," Grace said. "The other stores are killing us. Looks like we'll end up with lumps of coal in our stockings."

"It's not my fault," I insisted.

"Yeah, Haley, it kinda is," she said, and turned to wait on a customer.

Jeanette walked by with the guy she'd been talking to in the hallway. They exchanged a few more words, and he left. Jeanette spotted me. Her already sour expression worsened until she looked like the remains of a fruit basket two weeks after Christmas.

"We're far, far behind all the other stores in this contest, Haley. We have a lot of ground to make up," she said. "We desperately need those actresses back in the store to talk with our customers about charitable donations."

"Can't you just hire new actresses?" I asked.

"Word has gotten out about the murder," Jeanette said, and narrowed her eyes at me. "No one will work here."

I couldn't think of anything to say to that.

"The two actresses have far out-performed our own employees," she said. "You and the other girls who are filling in as elves are going to have to push much, much harder for donations, if we're to have any chance of a respectable showing in this contest."

I thought of a comeback but didn't say it aloud because I needed to keep this job.

Sleeping with the store owner will only get me so far.

"Are you following our customer service guidelines and asking every customer to donate to our children's charity drive?" Jeanette asked.

"See for yourself," I said, and held out the booklet Grace had just handed me. "I had to come back for a new booklet."

Jeanette glared at me like she didn't believe me, or something. I thought it best to change the subject.

"Who was that guy you were just talking to?" I asked, my mind spinning, trying to recall where I'd seen him. "Did he used to work here?"

"He's Trent Daniels, the boyfriend of that girl who was murdered," Jeanette said. "The one *you* found in the stockroom."

Jeez, was absolutely everybody ticked off at me for finding McKenna's body? Wasn't wearing this elf costume punishment enough?

I hate my life.

"He's completely devastated," Jeanette went on, like that was my fault, too. "He wanted to know if he could see the stockroom where her body was found."

My brain cells finally locked onto the reason Trent looked familiar to me. I'd seen him in one of the photos in Jasmine's apartment. He was standing in the background looking on as McKenna danced.

"I had to refuse his request, of course," Jeanette said, just as if I was interested. "Can you imagine the—the trauma that might have resulted?"

Trauma was code for *lawsuit* , of course.

"I have to get to work," I said to Jeanette, and walked away.

I was, of course, in no hurry to do any actual work. I wanted to catch Trent Daniels and talk to him about McKenna.

This morning when I'd spoken with Detective Shuman he'd been all about the money McKenna would earn from her role in the sitcom. Even though I knew more was going on with her personal life, I figured Shuman had a point.

Nobody I'd spoken to so far had any info on how McKenna had gotten the role. It seemed kind of weird to me that she hadn't told everyone. But I figured she'd told her boyfriend—and hopefully, he'd actually listened.

By the time I made it to the front of the store, there was no sign of Trent. I dashed to the door and spotted him pulling away in a Honda Civic.

No way was I running outside to flag him down wearing this elf costume.

"Hi, Haley," Sandy called.

I saw her standing by the fake fireplace while customers filled out the entry forms for the contest. I walked over.

"I'm glad you're still speaking to me," I said.

"You're my friend," Sandy told me. "Even if you did ruin our chances of winning those great prizes in the contest."

Oh my God, now even one of my closest Holt's BFFs was blaming me.

At this point, there was nothing to do but tell an all-out, shame-on-me-but-I'm-desperate lie.

"I think the police are closing in on the killer, and that means the actresses will come back," I said. "McKenna's boyfriend was just here talking to Jeanette."

"Really?" Sandy's face lit up.

"I'm pretty sure he told her the good news," I said. "He just walked past. Did you see him? The guy in the jeans and the Brooks & Dunn T-shirt."

Sandy's smile faded and she looked a little confused.

"That was McKenna's boyfriend?" she asked. "Are you sure?"

I got a weird feeling.

"Absolutely," I said. "Why?"

"He was in the store the other day. I remember because I saw his tat," Sandy said and touched the back of her neck. "It's a big gold star."

I hadn't noticed a tattoo on Trent, but Sandy's boyfriend was an ink artist so she paid attention to that sort of thing.

"He had on a Santa suit," Sandy said. "It was the first day of the sale. The morning McKenna was murdered."

Chapter 8

Now I had two absolutely-for-sure suspects, and one kind-of suspect.

I went to the Shoe Department stockroom, ignoring customers with ease, and closed the door behind me. I needed time to think about my suspects which, since the murder had happened in Holt's, technically meant that I was working.

Jasmine was my first suspect. I didn't want her to be guilty because I liked her. She was trying really hard to live her dream, and had a lot working against her.

But I couldn't shake the fact that she'd avoided my questions about why she hadn't showed up to work at Holt's the day of McKenna's murder, if she was really so desperate for money. Likewise, she hadn't told me whether or not she'd actually come to the store that morning.

It seemed like Jasmine had a good reason to want to keep McKenna alive in the hope of finally getting her back-rent. But maybe McKenna had told her she'd never pay her, even after those big fat sitcom paychecks finally rolled in. From what I'd heard about McKenna, she was moving ahead with her life and not looking back.

Trent Daniels also made a good suspect. Yeah, he really loved McKenna, according to everybody who'd talked to him—including Detective Shuman. But if he'd found out she was just using him for a free place to stay and thought she'd dump him as soon as she started collecting her twenty-thousand-dollar paychecks, maybe he'd gotten angry. Maybe he'd snapped—Shuman had said there was something weird about the guy. Plus, according to Sandy, Trent was in the store at the time of McKenna's murder, disguised in a Santa costume. Showing up this morning, acting all brokenhearted in front of Jeanette, asking to see the stockroom might have been a way to throw suspicion off of himself.

I'd seen the back door to the stockroom open that morning. Jasmine or Trent could have slipped in, murdered McKenna, then left totally unnoticed.

Alyssa ranked kind of in the middle on my personal rate-a-murder-suspect scale. She'd talked trash about McKenna every chance she got, and seemed way interested in Detective Shuman's investigation—almost *too* interested. These were sort of lame reasons to consider her a full-on suspect, so I put her in my mental kind-of suspect category.

Of course, a motive would be nice.

I paced around the stockroom, thinking hard, trying to come up with something—jeez, I could really use a Snickers bar right now. A chocolate-coated brain boost couldn't hurt.

There had to be some reason McKenna had been murdered. Who would want her dead?

Yeah, she'd skipped out on rent, used a guy who probably loved her for a free place to crash, and alienated everybody around her by bragging about her sitcom role. This made her a crappy person, and an even crappier friend and girlfriend. While some people probably wished McKenna were dead, I didn't see where any of this would cause someone to actually murder her.

I kept coming back to the rent McKenna owed Jasmine. Maybe Shuman was right. Maybe this whole thing was all about money.

I knew just who to ask.

I left the stockroom and successfully avoided two customers— one of which actually yelled for me, which was way rude, if you ask me—and circled the store until I spotted Nikki in ILA—retail speak for the Intimates, Lingerie and Accessories Department. I ducked down behind a rack of demi-cup, wireless push-up bras while she talked to a customer, then strolled over.

"Hi, Nikki," I said. "How's it going?"

"Cool," she said, and held out her charity donation booklet. "Look. I've gotten like ten donations this morning already. I just walked up to the customers and asked for a donation, and they all wanted to contribute."

Wow, how weird was that?

"They all loved that 'ho-ho-Holt's-for-the-holidays' line," she said.

Crap. That stupid marketing phrase. I still wasn't saying it—no matter how many donations I might get.

"I was thinking about what a tough break it was for McKenna," I said, "getting the big role, then getting killed."

Yeah, I know, I'd hit her with a hard topic without any sort of transition, something I'm sure all the top-rated detectives frowned on. But considering that Nikki was actually talking to customers, I couldn't take a chance that we'd be interrupted.

"Wow, yeah," Nikki said. "Like maybe they'll make a movie out of it, or something."

"How did she get the role?" I asked.

Nikki shrugged. "I don't know. She never said. I just saw it on her Facebook page one day. Getting the role was a super-big deal. She didn't even have an agent or anything."

"How could she get a part like that without an agent?" I asked.

Nikki thought for a minute. "Maybe she won a contest."

Now I was really confused.

"Production companies hold contests for roles?" I asked.

"Sometimes agents, casting directors, and producers will hold a contest on Twitter. It's sort of like their way of giving back to the industry and helping actors who are struggling," Nikki said. "You know, they tweet that the fiftieth—or whatever—person who tweets back will get a meeting, one-on-one, where they can ask questions and get personal advice. It's way cool. Alyssa won a meeting with a producer once."

I could imagine how fabulous face-time with a Hollywood insider would be to an aspiring actor.

"So did Alyssa get offered a great role or something?" I asked.

"I don't think so, but I'm not sure. I just heard about it from somebody else," Nikki said. Her usual perky smile faded a little. "Alyssa's been around for a long time, you know, trying to break in. She's older than she looks. She's like twenty-five already, or something. You know, she's really getting up there."

Nikki thought twenty-five was old? *I'll* be twenty five in a few months. Yikes!

Nikki leaned in a little. "I think Alyssa is getting kind of desperate. Last year she shaved her head for a role."

"She shaved her head?" I might have shouted that.

"Yep," Nikki said. "And they only paid her a thousand dollars."

"One lousy thousand dollars?" I'm sure I yelled that.

Oh my God. I couldn't believe somebody would actually do that. I would never be that desperate—not even for a Breathless satchel. *That's* how I feel about my hair.

"So, I don't know, maybe McKenna won a contest and whoever she met with got her the role," Nikki said. Her gaze wandered off, then came back to me. "There're some customers by the panties. Do you want to ask them about the charity donation?"

"The what?"

Nikki held out her booklet. "The charity donation for children."

I was way too traumatized by that whole head-shaving thing to wait on customers. I walked away, forcing the image from my mind.

I could really use a mocha frappuccino right now to steady my nerves.

Trent Daniels popped into my head. Of my two yeah-they-really-could-have-done-it suspects, and my one I'm-suspicious-but-don't-have-any-actual-reason-to-be suspect, Trent was the only one

I hadn't spoken with yet. Shuman had told me he'd talked with him already and had picked up some weirdness but not a he-did-it vibe, but I didn't know whether Shuman had brought up McKenna's big sitcom break.

I paused near the racks of greeting cards. Maybe I should call Shuman and suggest he talk to Trent about it, see if he would admit that McKenna was going to dump him and move out. But Shuman might not appreciate my oh-so fabulous suggestions on how to conduct his investigation—which I totally didn't get—plus, he could have already thought of that, and I didn't want to look like a moron if he had.

That meant I would have to talk to Trent myself. I didn't have any contact info for him, but I figured I could find him on Facebook.

I glanced around and didn't see any other employees—being really tall helps when I'm in stealth mode—so I slipped through the double doors into the stockroom.

Not a creature stirred back here, as usual. Just to make sure I wasn't interrupted—which is code for *caught*—I hurried up the big concrete staircase as fast as my pointed-toe elf shoes allowed and dashed between the huge shelving units to the back corner where the lingerie was kept.

I pulled my cell phone from my pocket and logged onto Facebook. Of course, there were more Trent Daniels listed than lights on the Rockefeller Plaza Christmas tree, but I finally found him. I messaged him, explaining that I was a friend of Nikki and Alyssa—which was kind of true—and asked him to contact me about McKenna.

I took a minute to check out his wall. Wow, this guy loved photos. He had a zillion pictures, one for every moment of his life for the past several years, it seemed.

A photo caught my attention. It was the one of McKenna I'd seen in Jasmine's apartment, where McKenna was dancing and everybody else was standing around watching. Only this picture was different.

Trent must have Photoshopped it because now he was no longer standing in the background. He was on the dance floor with

McKenna, and she was gazing up at him like she was having the time of her life.

Okay, that was kind of creepy.

Obviously, Trent loved Facebook. Not only did he post photos, it seemed he also posted absolutely every thought that went through his head.

Until this morning, that is.

He'd posted that he intended to go to Holt's and see where McKenna had died—which was kind of sad provided, of course, that he hadn't actually murdered her, as I suspected—but nothing after that.

Huh. I wasn't sure what that meant. Was he too distraught to comment on his visit? Or was something else going on?

I headed through the stockroom toward the staircase and my cell phone vibrated. My heart did its maybe-it's-Ty flutter, followed immediately by the all-too-familiar it's-probably-not-Ty thud.

It was Jasmine.

"Does your friend want to look at my apartment?" she asked, when I answered. "The first of the month is coming up fast."

She sounded kind of desperate, which didn't make me feel all that great about lying to her about knowing a possible roommate for her. Yeah, okay, I suspected her of murder—but I still felt bad for her.

"She's definitely interested," I said.

If Santa was really watching, I knew which of his lists he'd just put me on.

"But she's looking at another place, too," I said, thinking it might cushion the blow when my imaginary friend never materialized.

"Oh."

I pictured Jasmine slumping into despair, visions of Kia-dealership-guy and Scottsdale dancing in her head.

Not a great feeling.

"Why don't you come work here at Holt's?" I told her. "The store manager is desperate for more elves."

"I'm working on *The Closer* for the next four days," she said.

Jasmine sounded really down, so what better time to take advantage of the situation for my own benefit?

"So how come you didn't show up for the elf job at Holt's?" I asked.

I'd asked her this at her apartment and she'd evaded my question, distracting me with that rant about her mom. Maybe listening to her answer without getting caught up in her performance would be better.

"I *did* show up," Jasmine told me.

I gasped. She'd been at the store? The morning of McKenna's murder?

"I couldn't stand to look at McKenna's face, after she ditched me owing rent," Jasmine said. She sounded angry now. "So when I got to the store and she was there, I took off."

"Nobody saw you," I said, thinking of how both Alyssa and Nikki had said they hadn't seen her that morning.

"Because everybody—especially McKenna—was busy looking at themselves in the mirror," Jasmine told me, her voice rising. "I just took off. I ran into the stockroom and out the back door, because I knew if I stayed and McKenna said one word to me, I'd kill her."

Silence. Neither of us spoke. A really long couple of minutes dragged by.

Finally, Jasmine said, "Look, I didn't mean I would really kill McKenna. I just meant that I was mad at her."

"Sure. I understand," I said.

People said that sort of thing all the time. It didn't mean anything—usually. But Jasmine had just admitted that she'd been in the stockroom—the scene of the murder.

At least now I knew why the stockroom door was open. What I still didn't know was a motive for Jasmine—or anyone—to have killed McKenna.

"Tell your friend that if she wants the room, I need to know soon.   Otherwise, I'm going to have to find somebody else," Jasmine said, and hung up.

I tucked my phone into my pocket and went downstairs not feeling all that great.   I *really* didn't want Jasmine to be the murderer. And I *really* didn't want her to have to move back home.

Somehow, I was going to have to find her a roommate—if she didn't wind up in prison, that is, where she wouldn't have to worry about rent.

When I got down to the first floor, I left the stockroom through the double doors near the lingerie department.

"This is b.s.," somebody grumbled.

I spotted Bella standing in the next aisle. Beside her was a U-boat. Empty boxes were piled up around her.

In keeping with the Holt's Summer Santa Sale theme—and to avoid wearing the mandated Santa hat, no doubt—today she'd sculpted her hair into the shape of reindeer antlers.

I walked over.

"It's all b.s.," Bella said, slicing open the last box. She pulled out a wreath decorated with fake, sparkly fruit and a yellow bow. "In a few days, I'm going to have to put all this stuff back in boxes, and carry it all back to the stockroom—until *real* Christmas, when I'll have to haul it all out here again."

"It's b.s., all right," I said.

"And we're not even going to win a prize in the contest, because of you finding that dead elf," Bella said, and hung the wreath on the display rack.

Jeez, now my very best Holt's BFF was blaming me?

"It's not my fault," I told her. "If the employees want to be mad about something, they should be mad about having to wear those Santa hats. Everybody is going home with hat-hair."

Bella paused and nodded. "Yeah, that's b.s., too."

She hung the last wreath, and I helped her stack the empty boxes onto the U-boat.

"Still, it'd be nice to win a prize. You know, like getting a real Christmas present," Bella said, and headed for the stockroom, pushing the U-boat ahead of her.

"I know what I'd like to have for Christmas," a man said.

That voice. I knew that voice.

Oh my God. It was Jack Bishop.

I spun around and there he stood looking way hot in khaki cargo pants, boots, and a navy blue I-work-out-all-the-time-and-it-shows polo shirt.

His gaze traveled from my head to my toes, then back again.

"Yep, I know what's topping my wish list this year," he said.

Then I realized—*oh my God*—I had on that ridiculous elf costume.

I wanted to drop into a hole. Or maybe die. No, wait—I wanted to drop into a hole *and* die. I couldn't believe that hotter-than-hot Jack had seen me looking like this.

I hate my life.

"What was that all about?" he asked, nodding toward Bella as she disappeared into the stockroom.

He looked me up and down again, and his eyes got a smoldering look in them. Jeez, did he actually think I looked *good* in this costume?

Men are so weird sometimes.

"Exactly what kind of prizes are you giving out?" he asked. "I'm definitely interested in claiming some for myself."

A warm shiver went through me. Oh my God, only Jack can make a stupid Holt's contest seem sexy.

I thought it best to stick to the facts.

"It's this contest we're having," I said. "We're asking for donations from customers so Holt's can give presents to underprivileged children at Christmas."

Jack nodded. "Ho-ho-Holt's for the holidays."

Somehow that sounded cool when Jack said it. Still, there was no way I was uttering that phrase.

"And the employees of the store that gets the most donations win prizes," I said.

"Sounds like a good cause," Jack said. "How's it going?"

"Not all that great," I said. "We lost our professional elves and everybody blames me. So I have to wear this costume."

Jack grinned.

Jack's got a killer grin.

"You can count on me for a *big* donation," he told me.

He said that in his Barry White voice. I'm totally defenseless against his Barry White voice. My knees got weak.

Jack eased closer. He smelled really good.

"A huge donation," he said. "The biggest you've ever had."

Oh my God. I don't think Jack was talking about a monetary donation to the children's charity.

I'm pretty sure my heart actually stopped beating. I think I stopped breathing too—and forget thinking straight.

Then Ty popped into my head. *Now?* Now of all times, I thought about my official boyfriend—who was on the other side of the continent and hadn't called me since I don't know when?

I hate it when that happens.

Still, Ty was my official boyfriend. I was a real stickler about that sort of thing.

"So," I said, thinking it better to keep the conversation moving. "Are we still on for Saturday?"

Jack gave me one last smoking-hot look, then rolled with the change in topic.

"We're on," he said.

"How's Brooke?"

"She's a mess," Jack said.

"You're on the guest list for the charity event at the Stafford house," I said. "Your name is Jackson Blair. If anybody asks, you're an entrepreneur and philanthropist, and owner of Blair Group International in South Africa. Just tell everybody my mother invited you."

"Good cover," he said.

"You think we can really pull this off, right?" I asked.

"We?"

"I'll be there," I said, then realized I hadn't mentioned that Ty might be there, too—which was simply an oversight on my part. Really.

Jack gave me another one of his killer grins, and said, "Ho-ho-hold onto your Santa hat. Saturday night will be one hell of a sleigh ride."

Cool.

Chapter 9

"I've got some bad news," Nikki said.

Honestly, I didn't think more bad news could exist.

Marcie cancelled on me again last night—for a totally good reason, but still—so I didn't go shopping for a new gown to wear to the Staffords' party tonight. Yeah, okay, I could have called someone else or I could have shopped alone, but it's just not the same.

That meant I'd have to wear something I already owned. Not that I didn't have a perfectly appropriate dress—which meant that nobody who'd be at the event had seen me in it before—because I did. That wasn't the point. The point was that it's fun to go shopping for a special occasion with your BFF.

The only way I could possibly compensate for this disappointment was by carrying the Judith Leiber evening bag Jack had given me a few months ago—long story.

I still didn't know if Ty would make it back from New York in time to go to the party with me. Since he hadn't called, I had no way of knowing. True, I could have called him—again. But he knew about the event. I'd asked him to go. I'd texted him the info. No response.

In keeping with my own personal I'm-going-to-be-stubborn-even-if-nobody-gets-hurt-but-me policy, I just wasn't going to follow up with him. Of course, that meant I might end up walking into the Stafford home without a date, in full view of everybody who was super important, but I'd made up my mind. *That's* how annoyed I was with Ty.

Plus, I was supposed to go to my mom's house this afternoon to get ready for the party. It was a family tradition. Mom scheduled pedis, manis, massages, facials, and had a hairstylist come to her house and she, my sister, and I got ready together, then rode with the tuxedoed men in our lives in the limo mom also arranged.

Usually—well, sometimes—it was fun. But tonight my sister wouldn't be there, which meant I wouldn't be able to relax for a nanosecond—not with Mom peppering me with questions about when Ty would arrive, and fears that she'd actually looked at the party guest list she was responsible for compiling, spotted the name Jackson Blair, and would start asking questions.

Absolutely nobody at Holt's had spoken to me this morning. All I'd gotten from every single employee was double and triple stink-eye because our store was still in last place in the charity donation contest.

The shorts on my elf costume were still riding up. I had a major case of hat-hair, and now Nikki claimed there was more bad news.

I couldn't take it.

I walked off, leaving her in the Domestics Department. I desperately needed a Snickers bar from the vending machine in the breakroom—at the very minimum. Maybe I'd make a break for it and go to Starbucks. Yeah, that sounded way better.

"Haley, wait," Nikki called. She caught up to me and jogged alongside. "I think Alyssa is going to quit."

Oh, crap.

I stopped walking. Great. This was just what I needed to hear. One less elf to solicit donations. No way could the store boost itself out of last place if that happened. Plus, with Alyssa not on duty, Jeanette might want me to work double shifts in this wretched costume.

I hate my life.

"She can't quit." I might have said that louder than I should have.

Nikki shrugged. "She said she doesn't like it here."

"Nobody likes it here." I'm pretty sure I yelled that.

"I like it here," Nikki said.

Good grief.

"Tomorrow is the last day of the sale," I said. "Alyssa can hang that long, can't she?"

She made an it's-my-fault face, and said, "I think I made her mad."

Nikki was a sweetheart. I couldn't imagine her doing anything to upset Alyssa—unless she mentioned that whole it's-all-over-by-age-twenty-five thing, and then I couldn't blame her for being mad.

"What happened?" I asked.

"Well, you remember what you asked me yesterday?" she said.

Crap. Now I was going to get blamed for this, too?

"You know," Nikki said, "when you asked about how McKenna got that sitcom role? And I said maybe she won a contest? And then you asked how that worked? And then I said that Alyssa had won a contest? And then you asked—"

"Yeah, yeah, okay, I remember," I said.

"Well, so I got to thinking about it," Nikki said. "Like I was wondering what happened at the meeting she won. So I asked her, and she got mad. I mean like my-friend-borrowed-my-favorite-outfit-and-looks-better-in-it kind of mad."

Wow, that was seriously mad, all right.

"What did Alyssa say?" I asked. "Exactly."

"She said that what happened with the contest was nobody's business," Nikki said. "She said that I shouldn't have been talking to you about her. She said she'd seen you talking to that detective guy, and that she thought you were trying to blame her for McKenna's murder."

"What?"

"Yeah, that's what she told me," Nikki said. "I guess Alyssa is really sensitive about that contest she won and the meeting she had, because nothing came of it and, well, McKenna got a great role and nobody even knows why—like she wasn't even trying, or something."

"And Alyssa is trying really hard," I said.

"For a long time." Nikki cringed. "She's like really old now. Like almost—"

"Yeah, I got it," I said.

No way did I want to get into *that* conversation again.

"Anyway," she said. "I just thought you'd want to know since, well, Alyssa and I are just about the only people in the store still talking to you because you screwed up the contest for everybody."

"It wasn't my fault." I'm sure I yelled that.

Then I felt bad, of course, because Nikki was really trying to be nice to me.

"Thanks for letting me know," I said, and it came out sounding nice—considering.

Then something else popped into my head.

"You know Trent Daniels, don't you?" I asked.

"Sure. The guy who's lost his mind over McKenna," she said. "He's kind of weird."

"I messaged him yesterday, but I didn't hear back from him," I said.

She pulled her cell phone from her pocket and my day got a little boost seeing that Nikki had ignored the Holt's no-cell-phones-on-the-sales-floor policy. Maybe she and I could become kind-of BFFs.

"Wow, this is really strange," she said, shaking her head. "Trent hasn't been on Facebook since yesterday morning."

I remembered reading his last post before he came to the store to talk to Jeanette about seeing the stockroom.

I got a weird feeling.

Nikki dialed a number and held the phone to her ear. After a few seconds, she hung up and said, "His voicemail is full."

My weird feeling got weirder.

"Wow," Nikki said. "I hope he's okay."

I hoped he wasn't dead.

***

According to Nikki, Trent Daniels lived in Franklin Village in Hollywood. It was an older, established area of Los Angeles that had held up well over the years. There were tons of apartment buildings and houses—most of them built since back in the nineteen-twenties—squeezed into precious little space. Trees, shrubbery and flowering bushes filled every nook and cranny in between.

I'd been there with Marcie a couple of months ago. A friend of a friend had wanted to give a purse party so we'd stopped by her place to show her some of our bags. She loved them, of course, and ended up having a heck of a party—nothing says good-time like a couple dozen screaming women elbowing each other and stampeding toward a display table filled with knock-off designer handbags.

As soon as my shift had ended at Holt's I'd jumped in my Honda and headed south toward Los Angeles. I needed to talk to Trent and I was more than slightly worried that he seemed to have dropped off the grid yesterday.

I exited the 101 at Franklin Avenue, then hung a left on Tamarind Avenue. The place had a back-in-the-day vibe to it.

There were grocery stores, restaurants, coffee houses, all kinds of shops and businesses within walking distance.

Along with my concern for Trent, Alyssa had been on my mind. That whole conversation I'd had with Nikki this morning still bugged me. Why the heck would Alyssa think I was trying to pin McKenna's murder on her?

Yeah, okay, I did actually think she might be a suspect, but still.

Anyway, threatening to quit the elf job, getting mad at Nikki, and accusing me of trying to back-stab her with Detective Shuman seemed a bit over the top. Was Alyssa just being dramatic? Maybe. She was, after all, an actress.

Or like Jasmine, was this Alyssa's attempt at misdirection? Could be, since there was still that actress thing.

I guess I'd know for sure if I could come up with a motive for McKenna's murder.

Parking was at a premium, as in most of L.A., but I found an empty space at the end of the block and nosed into the curb. I got out and walked to Trent's apartment building. A few people were out, a mom pushing a stroller, a couple of girls with backpacks, a man carrying a grocery bag.

The building was pink stucco with a red tile roof. A patch of carefully manicured green grass was out front and vines climbed the walls. The entryway was kind of like a little tunnel that led past two of the first-floor apartments to a courtyard. In the center was a small pool, more grass, shrubs, and palm trees.

I climbed the metal staircase to the second floor and knocked on the door of apartment number 26. While I waited I looked over the railing at the pool. Six girls were stretched out on lounge chairs sunning themselves.

I knocked again and rang the bell.

The door next to Trent's opened and a guy with a messenger bag slung over his shoulder walked out. He was about my height, dressed in jeans and a black shirt that showed off his gym time, and looked unnaturally well groomed. I figured he was either an actor or a model.

"Have you seen Trent lately?" I asked. "I'm worried because his—"

"He keeps to himself. Everybody here keeps to themselves," he said, then cut around me and went down the stairs.

The guy didn't seem to have much going for him in the personality department. Good thing he was pretty, I guess.

I pounded on Trent's door and rang his doorbell about a dozen more times but still got no response, so I headed back downstairs and followed the signs to the manager's office. One of those fake clocks hung on the door, its hands indicating the manager was out and would return five minutes ago.

A girl waited nearby. I figured her for my age, tall, slender, wearing shorts, a tank top and flip-flops.

"She's still not back yet," she said, gesturing to the sign and looking a little annoyed. "If you're thinking about moving in here, get used to it. She's always off somewhere, doing something."

"Actually, I'm here to visit Trent Daniels," I said. "Do you know him?"

She drew back a little. "Are you a relative, or something?"

I'm not sure why that mattered, but I rolled with it.

"No, nothing like that," I said. "A friend of his hadn't heard from him in a while, so I said I'd stop by and check on him. He didn't answer his door."

I saw no reason to get into the whole his-girlfriend-was-murdered-and-I-found-her-body thing.

"That guy is a total recluse," she said, then mumbled, "a psycho recluse."

Okay, here was a choice bit of info about Trent I hadn't expected.

"I don't want to say anything bad about your friend," she said, "but he's really weird.   He's always kind of hanging around, watching people, like some kind of crazy stalker. It's creepy."

This wasn't what I expected to hear about heart-broken Trent Daniels. Creepy, all right.

I nodded at the sign on the office door, and said, "I can't wait any longer. I'll come back later."

We exchanged a wave and I left. At the complex entrance, I took the staircase down to the underground parking garage. A couple dozen cars were squeezed into tiny spaces. The ceiling was low. Light filtered in from the exit ramp that led up to the street.

Luckily, parking slots were assigned. I found the one numbered 26 and saw a Honda Civic, the same car I'd seen Trent drive away in the day he'd come to Holt's and talked to Jeanette.

The garage stunk like oil and gasoline, so I jogged up the exit ramp, and walked down the block to my car. Before I got in, I looked back at the apartment building, thinking maybe Trent would suddenly appear.

Since his car was here, he probably was, too, but there could be a lot of reasons he hadn't answered the door. Maybe he was in the shower or taking a nap. Maybe he had his iPod cranked up, or he was zoned out playing World of Warcraft.

Or he could have been lying inside dead.

I pulled out my cell phone and called Detective Shuman. His voicemail picked up. I'd rather have talked to him in person—strictly to insure that my information was passed along in a clear, concise, comprehensible way, that would maximize my effort to assist law enforcement, of course—but I didn't want to wait until I could catch Shuman in person. It was Saturday. Maybe he was out doing some fun girlfriend-boyfriend thing.

Jeez, I wonder what that would be like.

I left a message detailing my concern that Trent hadn't been heard from since visiting the store in an attempt to see the location of McKenna's murder. I also mentioned that Trent had a crazy-psycho-stalker reputation among the girls at his apartment complex and maybe speeding up his background check might be a good idea.

I hung up and gazed down the block at the building. I imagined Trent skulking around, lurking in the shadows, spying on the girls who lived here.

McKenna popped into my head.

Honestly, after hearing how Alyssa, Nikki, Jasmine, and some of the other actresses had talked about McKenna, I hadn't thought very highly of her.

Now I could only imagine how desperate she must have been for a place to live if she'd moved in with Trent.

Chapter 10

All of us looked great, if I do say so myself, as we rode in the limo to the Stafford house for the Christmas charity event.

Mom had on a silver Gucci gown which she'd accessorized with ruby jewelry. In true former beauty queen form, her hair and makeup were perfect. She could have—and would have—hit a runway somewhere with minimal prompting.

Dad looked dignified and handsome in his tuxedo.

I wore a red strapless gown with a sweetheart bodice. I didn't have a lot of expensive jewelry but I carried my Judith Leiber bag, which was more than enough to make everyone at the Stafford party jealous.

Ty had on—well, I didn't know what Ty had on because he wasn't there. I didn't know where he was. He'd texted me earlier and said that he'd meet me at the party.

Either Mom hadn't noticed he wasn't in the limo with us, or she'd simply accepted the explanation I'd given her because she hadn't grilled me about his absence. Instead, she filled our drive-time with speculation about who would be at the party, what they'd be wearing, and blah, blah, blah. I drifted off. I'm pretty sure my dad did, too.

Back about a hundred years ago, Orange Grove Boulevard had been home to wealthy families who built spectacular mansions and palatial houses, and surrounded them with lush landscaping, intricate gardens, pergolas, fountains, and palm, magnolia, hemlock, and cedar trees. Most of the huge houses had disappeared—along with the families and their money—replaced by smaller homes, apartments, and condos.

A few of the grand estates remained. The Stafford house was one of them. The place looked like an old Southern mansion, white with big columns rising to the roofline. It sat on two acres of carefully tended grounds.

I'd been here lots of times when I was a kid. My parents traveled in the same social circle as the Staffords, plus my older brother was around the same age as their son Chris. The Staffords had hosted Easter egg hunts, Fourth of July, and Christmas parties for us kids.

Our limo pulled into line with the other Towne Cars, Jags, Bentleys, and Mercedes and we crept slowly up the circular driveway. Even though it was summer and not quite dark yet, it looked as if jolly old Saint Nick might arrive at any moment.

Tiny twinkle lights covered the hedges and shrubbery, and were wrapped around the towering palm trees. Santa Claus stood by a sleigh, waving as cars drove past. An ice rink had been set up, surrounded by lush greenery. Skaters wearing red plaid costumes and ear muffs glided across the ice. A troupe of acrobats dressed in elf costumes performed stunts amid a stack of huge, gift-wrapped packages.

A sea of potted poinsettia plants covered the wide steps that led to the entrance of the house and a huge wreath hung above the door. A half-dozen carolers dressed in Old English costumes sang holiday songs.

Valets in red vests descended on our limo. Mom took Dad's arm. I followed them inside.

Two women welcomed us while another woman consulted the guest list—just why Mom wasn't handling this duty, I didn't know, except that her idea of taking charge of something really meant finding someone capable to whom it could be delegated.

It was really for the best.

I figured the women in the reception line for somewhere on the high side of sixty. None of them seemed to realize the fashion clock hadn't stopped in the eighties. The three of them standing together looked like the Battle of the Big Hair.

I wondered if Jack had arrived yet, but since I was in stealth-mode big-time, I couldn't lean over and check out the list.

The foyer and spacious living room were a crush of elegant gowns and tuxedos, a tribute to capitalism at its designer best. The women wore traditional Christmas colors of red, green, blue, gold, or silver. There were lots of pretend hugs and air kisses, everyone careful not to create a wrinkle or a makeup smudge.

The Staffords—or more likely the Staffords' servants and the design company they'd hired—had gone all out decorating the house for the occasion. Lighted trees and elegant displays of all things Christmas were in every room. Strains of music from a string quartet wafted above the conversations of the guests.

Mom and Dad were immediately sucked into the crowd. I made a break for the bar.

Laughter drew me down the hallway to one of the Staffords' massive sitting rooms were a bar had been set up. Guests were packed in there like toys in Santa's bag on Christmas Eve night. I made my way to the bar and asked for a glass of red wine. The bartender passed it to me just as a hard body eased up against mine.

Ty flew into my head—then out again just as quickly. He was my official boyfriend and we'd been doing the mattress mambo for a while now, so I knew whoever was brushing against me definitely wasn't Ty.

I looked over my shoulder. Jack Bishop.

I lingered for a few seconds—which was really bad of me, I know—then stepped away. It wasn't easy, but *that's* how serious I am about having an official boyfriend.

Not that he was here to notice, of course.

Jack gave me a little grin. My knees wobbled.

Oh my God. He looked insanely handsome in his tuxedo.

"Good evening, Miss Randolph," he said, and signaled the bartender for a bourbon on the rocks.

Oh, wow. This was so cool. We were in private-detective-mode already.

"Jackson Blair," I said. "Glad you could make it."

He took his drink, then rested his hand—it was really warm—on the small of my back. We wove through the crowd and found a spot near the doorway.

"I see you dressed for the occasion," he said, dipping his gaze to take in my gown.

"Red seemed appropriate," I said.

"You look like a Christmas gift," Jack said, and eased a little closer. "A gift that should be unwrapped ... very slowly."

My stomach got all warm and gooey.

I thought it better to change the subject.

"How's Brooke doing?" I asked.

Jack sipped his drink. "Not so good."

"She must be excited about what you're doing tonight," I said.

"She doesn't know."

It took a few seconds—my brain function seemed to have slowed down for some reason—to understand what he meant.

"You don't want Brooke to get her hopes up," I said, "in case you don't get the results you want tonight."

Jack angled closer. "I'll get what I want tonight."

He was making it really tough for me to stay in private-detective-mode.

I took a step back and said, "So what's the plan?"

Jack patted the pocket of his jacket. "I'll get video, enough to prove the little girl is in the house."

"Security?"

"Guards are still patrolling the grounds, discreetly, but none are in the house," Jack said. "They would be noticed. Guests would comment, ask questions. The Staffords want everything to seem perfectly normal."

"When are you doing it?" I asked.

"Right away," Jack said.

I figured it would be better to wait until later in the evening, when the guests all had a little more to drink and were hunkered down, distracted by conversations with friends. But I could see that Jack had a point, too. Better to get in and out quickly before suspicion was aroused in any way.

"Do you know how to get to the nursery?" I asked.

Jack shrugged. "Follow the trail of toys."

If that was Jack's plan, I saw a gaping hole in it. I'd told him at the restaurant on the night I met Brooke that this house was huge. I figured he'd pull the building plans from the county records, or something, but I guess he hadn't.

"It's not that easy," I said. "The house was built back in the day when rich people were paranoid about their kids getting kidnapped. The nursery is on the third floor. It's a maze. I know because we used to play hide-and-seek up there."

I got Jack's little grin again.

"Then you'll have to come with me," he said.

Oh my God. This was way cool—no, it was way cooler than cool. Jack wanted me with him on a covert op.

Where was my best friend when I needed her? I absolutely *had* to tell Marcie right away. But I held back. The mission came first.

Immediately, a plan flashed in my mind—which was kind of surprising, considering I hadn't had any chocolate since arriving and only a half glass of wine.

"The house has three staircases," I said. "We'll use the one near the kitchen."

"After you," Jack said, gesturing with his hand.

We left our glasses with a passing waiter and I led the way past the living room and foyer, toward the east wing of the house. The place was packed with people. The noise level had spun up considerably.

The crowd thinned as we walked down the hallway past the entrance to the formal dining room. By the time we passed the family breakfast nook, the butler's panty and the kitchen, we encountered only the catering staff and none of them gave us a second look.

The staircase was steep and narrow, since it was designed to be used mostly by the house servants, and not all that easy to climb in a tight fitting gown, a strapless bra, and three-inch heels.

Jack trotted behind me, completely at ease, which was really annoying.

"You owe me," I said, trying desperately to control my breathing and not pant like a grandma at the Christmas closeout sale when we finally reached the third floor.

"Sounds fair," Jack said, still looking crisp and breathing normally. "How about I surprise you with something?"

"I want a Breathless handbag," I told him, and leaned against the wall—just to revitalize myself for the sake of the operation and not because I hadn't been to the gym in a week.

"You'll like my surprise better," he told me.

He braced both hands against the wall, locking me in front of him.

Jeez, I didn't remember it being so *hot* up here on the third floor.

"In fact," Jack whispered, "you'll like it two, maybe three times on the same evening."

I lost my breath completely.

A wild, crazy heat rolled off of Jack that made me think about doing wild, crazy things—which I would never do, of course, because I have an official boyfriend.

"The nursery is this way," I said.

I ducked under his arm and headed down the hallway.

Dim light radiated from a few wall sconces. The Oriental carpet runner and the wallpaper looked new.

Jack followed as I turned a corner, then another, went down a corridor, and turned yet another corner. Yeah, okay, at this point I didn't know exactly where I was, but, jeez, I hadn't been up here in years, and how the heck was I supposed to think straight with Jack close to me still radiating nuclear-grade heat?

He stopped and grabbed my hand, pulling me up short.

"Somebody's coming," he whispered.

I went still, straining my ears. "I don't hear—"

"Shh. Footsteps, getting closer."

I didn't hear anything, but that didn't stop me from going into panic mode.

Oh my God, we couldn't get caught up here. The Staffords would figure out what we were doing, they would move Hope, and Brooke might never get her back. Plus, I had an official boyfriend—who had become something of an inconvenience, but still—and I couldn't be seen lurking in an upstairs corridor, three floors away from the party, with a hot guy like Jack.

"We've got to hide." I might have said that a little louder than I should have.

"We'll hide in plain sight."

Jack hustled me into a corner and planted himself in front of me, completely blocking my view of the hallway. His hand settled onto the curve of my hip, his other spread across my cheek.

Oh my God.

He leaned down and whispered, "Nobody will say anything if they see us like this."

His breath was warm against my ear. Oh wow, he smelled great.

I felt his lips on my neck. His hand left my waist and crept higher.

Every thought flew out of my head—except one: I still didn't hear any footsteps.

Huh.

I put both palms against Jack's chest—he had really great muscles—and shoved him away.

"The nursery is this way," I said, and took off down the hallway.

The nursery was actually a suite of rooms, a bedroom for the nanny, a kitchenette, a bathroom, a play room, and two more bedrooms for children.

I stopped outside the doorway to the playroom. Jack took up a position across from me. Lights burned low inside.

The playroom was decorated in a jungle theme with a mural of friendly, laughing lions, giraffes, monkeys, and elephants painted on the walls. There was a bookshelf, a child-sized desk and chair, an easel, and a dozen bins filled with toys. It all looked new so I figured Alton and Sable must have had the room redecorated when Brooke started letting Hope visit them.

Since it was late, I figured the nanny had put Hope to bed already and was enjoying some personal time in her own room.

Jack pulled out his camera and activated its video feature. I stayed out of camera range as we crossed the playroom to a short corridor with several doors leading off of it. A beam of light shone from beneath one of the doors. The nanny's room.

Fainter light—probably from a night light—filtered from beneath the door across the hall. Jack slowly turned the knob and stepped inside. I leaned around him and saw a little girl lying in a canopy bed, sleeping soundly. She had on pink pajamas, and her curly blonde hair was splayed across a butterfly-print pillow.

I recognized her right away from the photo Brooke had showed me at the restaurant. It was Hope.

I wanted to grab her in my arms and run out of the house with her—which, I know, totally defeats the whole purpose of a covert op—but that's the way I felt.

Jack must have sensed it—or maybe he felt the same way—because he took my hand and pulled me out of the room. He kept his camera on as we left the nursery suite, went through the hallways, down the stairs, and back into the crowded party.

"Let's get out of here," Jack said, tucking his phone into his pocket.

He was in private-detective mode now, his mission accomplished, anxious to make a quick exit with his prize intact.

"I took a car service here, but I left a car down the block," Jack said, as we made our way through the crowd.

We slipped past the ladies still welcoming guests to the party and went out onto the porch. It was dark now. The tiny golden lights in the shrubbery twinkled. The line of arriving cars had trickled to a few.

One of them was a totally hot Porsche 911 Turbo.

I knew that car.

It pulled to a stop and the valet opened the door. Ty got out.

I looked around for Jack.

He was gone.

Chapter 11

"Aren't you coming in?" I asked.

I'd just opened the door to my apartment but Ty hadn't followed me inside.

He glanced at his watch. Not a good sign.

We'd driven back to my place from the party at the Stafford home. It had taken all the patience I could muster—and, really, I didn't have all that much to begin with—to stay at the party, circulate among the guests and make small talk.

I'd been totally freaked out that somehow Alton and Sable Stafford would find out that I'd been upstairs with Jack shooting video of their granddaughter, would sound some kind of silent alarm, and all the doors and windows in their huge house would somehow slam shut holding me captive until the cops showed up.

Not a great feeling.

"I have a conference call with Tokyo tonight," Ty said.

This wasn't a great feeling either. Apparently, Ty had squeezed my request to attend the Stafford party in between a meeting in New York and a telephone call.

But, at least, he'd come to the party. I guess I should be happy about that. And he did look smoking hot in his tuxedo.

I looped my arms around his neck.

"You can come back after your conference call," I suggested.

Ty drew me closer. It felt really good.

"I have to fly out first thing," he said. "I'm personally awarding prizes to the store that finishes in first place for our charity drive."

Oh, crap. That contest. Talk about a mood killer.

"We'll know the official winner at close of business tomorrow—well, today, technically," Ty said. "But one store is way out in front."

Since I knew it couldn't possibly be my store, I didn't ask which one it was.

That, however, didn't stop Ty from blabbing on about it.

"So it looks like I'll be in San Francisco," he said.

I couldn't think of anything to say to that, and since I didn't want to hear anything more about Holt's—plus my feet hurt and I was six hours into a four-hour dress—I said, "I guess I'll see you whenever."

Ty tilted my face up to his. "You could come with me. There's lots of great shopping in San Francisco."

Yeah, that sounded great. But sitting around a hotel room, waiting for Ty to finish his meetings and actually show up, didn't.

"I have to work tomorrow," I said.

"You could take the day off," he said.

"So could you."

We just looked at each other for a few seconds, then Ty grinned.

"You're being stubborn," he said.

Like I didn't already know that.

"Do you think I invite just *anybody* to spend the night with me?" I asked.

The playful look disappeared from his face.

"No, Haley, I don't think that at all," he said. "But I have responsibilities. You know that."

Yes, I knew that.   And I was getting a little tired of being reminded.

"I'll arrange something special for you when I get back," Ty said. "It will be great. You'll love it."

"Do you plan to go with me?" I asked.

He chuckled. "You can count on it."

I gave him a kiss—just so he'd know what he was missing out on tonight—and he left.

I closed the door, kicked off my shoes and headed for the bedroom. A knock sounded on the door.

My heart fluttered—but not in a good way.

Ty. He'd changed his mind. What nerve.

Yeah, okay, just a minute ago I'd practically put the smack down on him to not leave, but now I was a little more than slightly annoyed that he hadn't. He thought he could just change his mind, come back, and it would be okay?

I stomped across the room and yanked the door open, ready to give Ty a huge piece of my mind.

Only Ty wasn't standing there.

It was Trent Daniels.

Oh, crap.

"Hi, Haley," he said. "Can I come in?"

Oh my God. How did he know who I was? How did he know my name? How did he know where I lived?

And where were my official boyfriend and my smoking hot private detective at a time like this?

Trent looked bigger up close. He'd seemed tall when I saw him in the store, but now with him standing a couple of feet from me I could tell he was at least six-five. He had a lot of mass—not muscle—but it was still intimidating—especially at one o'clock in the morning, with the words *psycho stalker* blaring in my head, standing in the dark, on my doorstep, when all my neighbors were sound asleep and probably couldn't hear me scream.

"How did you find me?" I asked.

"You sent me a message," Trent said. "On Facebook."

Oh, yeah, that's right. I'd totally forgotten.

"But I didn't tell you where I lived," I said.

"Yeah, I know." He fidgeted for a few seconds, then said, "I followed you back from my apartment."

Oh my God.

"That was hours ago," I said. "Have you been waiting here all this time?"

"Kind of," Trent said.

He had on sweat pants, a stretched-out T-shirt and flip-flops. His hair hung over his forehead and I don't think he'd shaved in a couple of days.

I'm not sure how Trent put everything together—seeing me outside his apartment, reading my name on the message I'd sent him—but maybe he'd talked to Nikki or Alyssa and they'd filled him in.

Or maybe he'd figured it out online, somehow, like the other psycho stalkers did.

"When I saw you outside my apartment, I remembered you from the store so I thought you could answer some questions for me about McKenna," Trent said. "The cops, they won't tell me anything."

Trent sounded upset about McKenna's death. The other actresses had said he genuinely loved her.

Or maybe it was obsession.

"Where have you been?" I asked. "Nobody has seen or heard from you in a while."

He got a weird look on his face which creeped me out big-time.

"Is that why you came to my apartment?" he asked. "You were worried about me?"

"Lots of people were worried," I said.

Okay, that wasn't exactly true, but I thought it better to minimize my concern.

"I was too bummed out to talk to anybody," Trent said. "So what happened? How did McKenna ... die?"

This hardly seemed the best time to get into this kind of conversation, but I didn't know when I'd have a chance to talk to him again, so I rolled with it.

"Don't you know?" I asked. "You were in the store that morning."

"I thought it would be cool," he said. "McKenna told me she was going to wear an elf costume, so I figured I'd dress up like Santa, get our picture together. McKenna takes great pictures. Look."

He reached into his shirt pocket where I could see the outline of his cell phone, but no way did I want to amble down memory lane with him.

"So you saw McKenna that morning?" I asked.

Trent's face twisted into a frown. "I waited outside with the customers. I saw the elves inside, before the store opened, but I couldn't spot McKenna."

That was because she was already dead, stuffed inside the giant toy bag in the stockroom.

McKenna had been murdered before the store opened. Trent could have gone in through the rear door of the stockroom that Jasmine had left open, gotten McKenna to join him back there, killed her, then left through the same door and come around to the front of the store and hung out with the other customers.   It made for a pretty good alibi.

But why? Why would Trent have wanted McKenna dead?

"I heard McKenna was moving out of your place," I said.

"No way."

Anger bubbled up in Trent. He took a step toward me. I wanted to step back but didn't, since I figured he'd follow and that would put us both inside my apartment.

"Who told you that?" he demanded. He curled his hand into a fist and pounded it against his palm. "It was that bitch Alyssa, wasn't it? She was so jealous of McKenna. She got that great sitcom role, and Alyssa couldn't stand it."

My heart pounded harder in my chest. My mind whirled trying to think of how to get away from this guy. I knew I couldn't jump back, slam my front door and turn the lock before Trent pushed it open, and he was so big I couldn't dash around him and get away— not barefoot, wearing a floor-length gown.

Maybe instead of the Breathless purse I should have asked Jack for a gun.

I hope I still get a chance to do that.

"Getting that role was a big deal," I said, trying to calm Trent down. "How did McKenna manage it?"

"She met some big producer." Trent fumed for another few seconds, then smiled. "McKenna was so beautiful. The guy just loved her. He cast her right away. I've got a picture of it. I downloaded it off of her phone the other day. Want to see?"

Good grief. Enough with the pictures.

"So McKenna got a fantastic role, but Alyssa didn't," I said. "Sounds like Alyssa blew her big chance, all right."

"Damn straight."

"Must have been exciting," I said, "living with an upcoming big star, knowing you'd be going to premier parties, hanging out with celebrities."

Trent shook his head. "McKenna wasn't into all of that. She loved *me*."

From what the other actresses had said about McKenna, I doubted that was true. But this was hardly the time to mention it.

Trent seemed lost in thought for a minute to two, then said, "Can you tell me what happened to McKenna? You were in the store that morning, weren't you? Do you know?"

I never really understood why people wanted the sordid details surrounding the death of somebody they loved, but maybe knowing about those final minutes made them feel closer, somehow.

Maybe telling Trent something about that morning would make him feel better.

Maybe it would get him to leave.

But no way was I telling him that I was the one who'd found McKenna. I was far from convinced that Trent hadn't murdered her, and knowing that I'd witnessed the crime scene might make him think he had to murder me, too.

"I heard a few things mentioned in the store," I said. "She hit her head."

Trent flinched and rocked back a little, as if he could feel the same pain McKenna must have felt.

"Do you … do you think she suffered?" he asked quietly.

I flashed on the Christmas decorations that had been knocked onto the stockroom floor in what must have been one heck of a struggle, the heavy nutcracker she'd been struck with, the big pool of blood.

"No," I said. "I don't think so."

Trent just stood there for a few more minutes, then nodded.

"Thanks, Haley," he said. "Thanks for telling me. I won't forget you for this."

Oh, *please*, forget me.

He walked away, then stopped and turned back.

"I'll send you that picture," he said.

"Great," I said, then jumped back into my apartment, closed the door and turned the lock.

I drew in a couple of big breaths trying to calm down, then looked out the peep hole in my door.

No sign of Trent.

I hoped that meant he'd actually left and wasn't still hanging around out there.

Oh my God, I was so rattled. Nothing could help me now but my emergency bag of Oreos.

I got them from the top shelf of my kitchen cabinet and medicated my way through a half-dozen or so as I changed into my pajamas, combed out my hair, and washed off my makeup. I was too wound up to sleep, so I plopped down on my living room sofa to think.

Trent jumped into my head.

I hadn't heard back from Detective Shuman since I had left him a message after leaving Trent's apartment, voicing my concern that Trent's neighbors had put him in the possible-stalker-avoid-that-weirdo category. I wasn't sure if that meant Shuman had already checked into Trent's background and found nothing, and he hadn't bothered to call and tell me, or if perhaps he was too busy with other aspects of McKenna's homicide investigation.

Or maybe he was hanging out with his girlfriend.

I crammed two cookies into my mouth and re-focused my thoughts.

Trent seemed to genuinely believe McKenna loved him and was convinced she wouldn't have moved out after her big break. But I doubted that was true. I recalled how the elf actresses were talking about McKenna the morning I'd rounded them all up and brought them to the training room, before Jeanette had told them about McKenna's death. One of them had mentioned she was looking at condos on the beach.

If she really was planning to dump Trent and move out, maybe he'd found out. Maybe, as psycho stalkers were wont to do, he couldn't bear the thought of losing her so he killed her—which didn't make a lot of sense to me, but there it was.

It was the closest thing to a motive for McKenna's murder that I'd come up with so far.

I spun the top off of another Oreo, licked the icing, then shoved the cookie into my mouth.

If I needed a motive for someone simply *not liking* McKenna, it would be Alyssa. And, really, I couldn't blame her.

Alyssa had blown her big chance when she'd won that contest and met with a producer, while McKenna had made such a good impression she'd been cast practically on the spot. Envy and jealousy weren't uncommon in any profession, but even more so among actors. From what I'd seen, their lives were pretty tough. Financial problems, audition after audition, rejection after rejection. To be that close and not make it must have crushed Alyssa, especially because she'd been trying for so long—she was twenty-five years old, after all.

Plus, it seemed, McKenna hadn't been very gracious about winning the role. In fact, she'd been flaunting it to anyone and everyone within ear shot.

Had it been too much for Alyssa? Had she simply reached her boiling point with McKenna and lashed out?

And then there was that whole rent thing with Jasmine. Disputes over money had killed a lot of people.

I popped another cookie into my mouth.

Alyssa, Jasmine, and Trent had all been at the store that morning, but so far I hadn't uncovered a good reason for any of them to murder McKenna.

Crap.

Chapter 12

Since I knew I'd be out late at the Staffords' party last night, I scheduled myself for the late shift today at Holt's. For once, I was glad to be in the store—but only because this was the last time I'd have to wear this god-awful elf costume, and I was anxious to get the whole Summer Santa Sale thing over with.

Usually, the crowd slowed down as the day wore on, but not today. Customers pillaged and plundered the shelves and racks, desperate, it seemed, to max out their credit cards and overdraw their bank accounts while comforting themselves with the but-it's-a-great-price excuse, a personal favorite of mine.

The Summer Santa Sale was in its final death throes but none of the store management seemed ready to give up on it—or its contribution to their annual bonuses. The department managers had taken to the sales floor themselves, hitting up customers for donations to the children's charity.

Jeanette led the effort—which I didn't think really helped the cause. In keeping with her Christmas-themed attire, today she had on a brown pantsuit with, for no apparent reason, a huge red button at her throat.

She looked kind of like the Rudolph float in the Macy's parade.

"Hi, Haley," Nikki said, and walked up with her usual perky smile in place. "You look upset. Are you okay?"

Considering that Rita—I hate her—had assigned me to the Infants Department—I hate that department—and I had two more grueling hours to go wearing an elf costume, and almost nobody in the store was speaking to me, plus my boyfriend had ditched me last night and I'd been visited by a possible psycho-stalker, and I still hadn't figured out who had killed McKenna, I thought I was in pretty good shape.

Apparently, I wasn't pulling it off as well as I'd thought.

"Just a lot of stuff going on, that's all," I said.

Nikki nodded as if she knew exactly what I meant, though I sincerely doubted it.

"At least Alyssa came in today," she said, giving me a doesn't-that-make-it-all-better smile. "She's really good at getting donations. Maybe the store will finish in next-to-last-place instead of the very bottom."

Yes, that was something to look forward to, all right.

"It was fun working here," Nikki said.

She sounded as if she meant it and, honestly, Nikki had been really sweet. I liked her and I'd miss her.

"You'll probably be a big star next year," I said. "But just in case you're not, maybe you can come back and work the sale again."

"That would be so cool," Nikki said. She glanced off to the right and her eyes got big. "I see a customer."

She dashed away.

My day needed a boost. I desperately needed to talk to somebody who would take my mind off my problems—and a Snickers bar wouldn't hurt, either.

Marcie, my best BFF on the entire planet, sprang into my mind, along with the vending machine in the break room. With the blatant disregard for Holt's no-phones-on-the-sales-floor policy that I was known for, I pulled out my cell and headed for the rear of the store.

Bella stepped into the aisle from the Boys Department.

"It's b.s.," she said. "You ask me, it's b.s."

Even though Bella hadn't been tasked with wearing an elf costume, she'd kept up her commitment to holiday-hair right to the bitter end.   Today she'd fashioned what looked like a candy cane atop her head.

Bella looked mega annoyed about something, and I really had enough problems of my own.   But since she was one of the two people who'd spoken to me so far today, I stopped.

"What's up?" I asked, and tucked my cell phone into my pocket.

"That big sign in the break room," she said.

There was a sign in the break room?

"About the store meeting tonight," she said.

There was a meeting?

"Can you believe it?" Bella said.   "All the employees *have* to be there.   Jeanette is even calling employees who aren't working, telling them to come in."

Oh, crap.   This couldn't be good.

"We're probably going to have to sit there for an hour, getting yelled at because we did so bad in the contest," Bella said.

"That's b.s., all right," I said.

"Damn right it is," she grumbled, and walked away.

Well, that didn't exactly brighten my day.   Now I absolutely had to talk to Marcie.   I pulled out my cell phone again and—come on, really?—my day actually got worse.   Trent had texted me.

For a few seconds, I ignored it.   Then I thought that maybe this could be something good.   Maybe he'd texted me his confession.

I hit the view button on my cell phone and his message popped up.   Only it wasn't a message.   It was a picture of McKenna.

He'd tried to show it to me last night but I'd plowed ahead with questions, hoping to uncover some evidence in McKenna's death.   I guess Trent was just bound and determined I was going see the picture that had been taken at her big meeting with the Hollywood producer.

I ducked behind the greeting cards display rack and accessed the picture.

The photo had been taken outside on a restaurant patio. From the buildings in the background, I guessed it was in downtown L.A. somewhere. Bright sunshine filtered through vine-covered lattice work. The tables were covered with yellow linens, and set with floral china.

My heart did a little dip, seeing McKenna in the center of the shot, knowing she was dead now. Her arm was raised as she held up what I guessed was her phone to snap the picture of herself, on what had surely been the greatest day of her life.

She wore an emerald green tank top, accessorized with big, hoop earrings and a chunky necklace. A tote was slung over her shoulder, a yellow Fossil that I recognized from last winter.

The heart of the photo was McKenna's smile. It was brilliant.

Beside her stood a man I didn't recognize, but I figured he was the producer she'd met with. Fifty was in his rearview mirror, yet it was obvious he was fighting it. Fake tan, jaw line stretched a little too tight, not a gray hair in sight.

Behind McKenna, a waiter in a white shirt had gotten caught by the camera, and off to the side the arm of a woman carrying a Louis Vuitton satchel had made it into the shot.

Hang on a second.

I enlarged the photo and centered it on the satchel. The bag was a knock-off. I'd seen hundreds of counterfeits since Marcie and I had started our purse party business, but something about this one seemed different.

Handbags—dozens of them---flashed through my brain quicker than Santa Claus slid down a chimney. I'd seen this satchel some place before, very recently. It didn't have simply the exclusive LVT pattern the company was known for. It was mixed with their checkerboard design that—

Oh my God.

Alyssa had a satchel just like this.

Was the bag in the photo *her* bag?   If it was, how could that be?

Alyssa had won a contest and the opportunity to meet with a producer. Was the man in the picture standing next to McKenna that same producer?   And if he was, why was Alyssa there at McKenna's meeting?

Was it just a crazy coincidence?

I wasn't big on coincidences.

I accessed my phone book and punched Detective Shuman's name. He answered on the third ring.

"Where are you?" I might have said that kind of loud.

"Well, hello to you, too," he said and uttered a little laugh.

"Get here," I told him. "Now."

"What's wrong?" Shuman must have picked up on the oh-so subtle something-huge-happened urgency in my voice because he launched into cop-mode immediately.

"I'm at the store," I said.   "I think I know who murdered McKenna Crane."

***

Shuman insisted that I wait until he got here but, of course, no way was I doing that. The store would close in about an hour and that meant Alyssa would leave, and I couldn't let that happen. Plus, there was a chance that my suspicion was colder than Christmas day at the North Pole, and if I was wrong I wanted to know before Shuman showed up.

I circulated through the store searching for Alyssa and finally spotted her in the Women's Department. She looked up as I approached. Maybe she saw something in my expression. Maybe she figured her luck had run out. I don't know, but she left the department heading for the rear of the store. She went into the elves' dressing room. I followed her inside.

No one else was there. The place was cluttered with street clothes and shoes, makeup and hair care products. Alyssa retreated to the farthest corner of the room.

"I'm leaving early," she said, and ripped off her Santa hat.

"I don't get it," I said, because really, I didn't. "How did you end up at McKenna's meeting?"

Alyssa flattened herself against the wall, as if my words had blasted her onto it.

"I saw the photo McKenna took that day. You were there, too. How did you know she was meeting that producer?" I asked.

Alyssa pressed her lips together as if she were trying to hold back. Then, I guess, she'd held back too long already. Her eyes got wild, and she clinched her hands into fists at her sides.

"It wasn't *her* meeting! It was *mine*! I won that contest! I won that meeting! And McKenna crashed it!"

"She just showed up?" I asked.

"Yes! A bunch of us were all together, tweeting, trying to win, and I won!" Alyssa screamed. "Then when I got there, McKenna appeared out of nowhere. She took over. She threw herself at the producer—and she stole *my* chance at a huge role!"

"That was really crappy," I said.

"I've been at this forever. I finally—finally—got a break and she ruined it!"

Honestly, I couldn't blame Alyssa for being mad. McKenna had definitely back-stabbed her big-time.

"So that's why you killed her?" I asked.

"No." Alyssa shook her head. She drew in a couple of big breaths and calmed down a little. "I let it go. I was furious, but I let it go. I mean, I might not have gotten the role anyway, right? So I put it aside and moved on."

I believed that she'd moved on, like she said. But I figured that wasn't the end of it.

"But McKenna wouldn't let it go?" I asked.

Alyssa's cheeks turned red and her breathing became labored.

"She just wouldn't shut up about it," she said. "She kept shooting off her mouth about her *chance* meeting with a producer—she sure wasn't going to tell the truth and make herself look bad."

"I heard all the talk about how McKenna planned to get a personal assistant, a condo at the beach," I said which, under the circumstances, was super crappy of her. "I guess she was still talking it up that morning when you all came to work here?"

"Oh, you bet she was," Alyssa said.

"So you asked her to keep quiet?"

"I couldn't take it any more," she said, and tears sprang to her eyes. "When we were leaving the dressing room, I pulled her into the stockroom, and I told her that she could blab her big mouth all she wanted, but I knew the truth about what she'd done, and to keep quiet around me."

"That sounds reasonable," I said.

Where was Detective Shuman?

"She went crazy." Alyssa flung out her arms.

Why wasn't he here yet?

"She tried to leave the stockroom—like she was too good to talk to me," Alyssa said. "She pushed me."

I didn't need night vision goggles to see where this was going.

"So you pushed her back," I said.

"I would never have pushed her, if she hadn't pushed me first," Alyssa said. She was crying harder now. "And she stumbled against that big shelving unit, and knocked all the decorations into the floor, then she fell down, too."

McKenna hadn't died from a fall. She's been hit on the head. I knew something more than happened.

"It scared me," Alyssa said, swiping at her tears. "I thought she'd gotten hurt. I tried to help her up but she slapped me. She was so mad—like she couldn't believe something like that could actually happen to her. Like she was invincible now, since she'd gotten that big role."

Alyssa pressed her palm to her forehead and shook her head, as if she couldn't bear to remember what had happened.

"McKenna said I'd assaulted her," Alyssa said. "She said she was going to call the police and I'd be arrested. She said I'd be thrown in jail. She was going to get all kinds of publicity, and everybody in Hollywood would know what I'd done to her, and I'd never—ever—find work as an actress."

At that point, I might have hit McKenna, too.

"I couldn't let her do that." Alyssa shook her head frantically. "I don't know what happened. She just wouldn't shut up. And all I could think was that my career was *over*. I'd never, never, never be an actress."

"So you hit her on the head with the nutcracker," I said.

"It happened to fast." Alyssa gasped for air. "I don't know what I was thinking. She just wouldn't shut up. So I picked up that thing and I hit her with it."

We both went silent, Alyssa's panting the only sound in the room. Her eyes were focused on nothing but were filled with the horror of what she'd done that day.

After a couple of minutes, she looked up at me and said, "I never meant to hurt her. I certainly didn't mean to kill her."

"I understand," I said, because really, I did.

She hurried over to me. "You're not going to tell anyone, are you? You—you can't tell anyone. Please, you can't."

Maybe I wouldn't tell anybody.

For a few seconds I considered it. The whole thing was an unfortunate situation that got out of hand. Alyssa hadn't meant to hurt McKenna, and McKenna had definitely provoked her.

But, really, it wasn't my call to make.

Alyssa must have seen my decision flash across my face because she cut around me and ran out the door. I took off after her.

First of all, it's really hard to run in pointed-toed elf shoes. But the good part was that when customers saw two elves running all-out through the aisles, they got out of the way.

Alyssa sprinted past the checkout lines and blasted through the front doors. I followed.

Where was Shuman? Where was he when I called? Had he had time to get here?

I didn't see Shuman, but a black-and-white patrol car sat at the curb. Two officers were standing at the rear bumper waiting, I guessed, for him to show up.

"Hey!" I screamed.

The officers turned and saw me.

"Stop her!" I yelled, and pointed toward Alyssa who was heading into the parking lot.

One of them started after her. Wow, that guy ran really fast—which was way hot, of course. He caught her. She tried to wrestle away, then gave up and started crying.

I jogged over just as Detectives Shuman and Madison pulled up.

Chapter 13

Detective Madison looked disappointed, as usual, that I hadn't committed murder. He'd actually asked Alyssa—twice—if she'd really done it, even after she'd confessed to the two patrolmen and both him and Detective Shuman.

Everybody was loaded up into their cars, ready to pull away from the store, but Shuman held back.

"Sorry I sent you on that wild goose chase about Trent Daniels," I said.

"Your instincts were right-on," he said. "He had a juvenile record, sealed of course, but I talked to one of the guys who'd worked the case. Seems Daniels couldn't stop looking in his neighbors' windows."

Jeez, was I ever glad I'd never see that weirdo again.

"Good work," Shuman said, then gave me the once-over in my elf costume. "This puts you on Santa's 'nice' list, for sure."

"And what about you?" I asked. "Which list are you on?"

Shuman grinned. "I could work my way onto the 'naughty' list very easily."

A few 'naughty' thoughts sprang into my head—which was bad of me, I know—and from the look in Shuman's eyes, 'nice' wasn't on his mind, either.

Then we both snapped out of it.

"Someone will notify you if you're needed for follow up," Shuman said, and backed away.

"Whatever," I said, and headed back to the store.

Rita—I hate her—waited at the entrance, holding the door open and glaring at me.

"Could you move it a little faster, princess?" she said.

I slowed my pace considerably, then sauntered inside. She shut the door and locked it.

"You're supposed to be in the stockroom," Rita said. "Hurry up and get back there."

Since I wasn't in any great rush to get bitched-out by store management for our appalling performance in the children's charity contest—and I sure as heck wasn't going to wear this elf costume another second—I headed for the dressing room.

A few I'm-going-to-get-the-sale-price-no-matter-how-many-employees-I-have-to-inconvenience customers were in line. Most of the cashiers were closing their registers. The store lights had been turned down, but the Christmas trees were still lit.

I was the last elf in the dressing room. I changed clothes, re-applied my makeup, and was forced to compensate for a severe case of hat-hair by pulling it up into a ponytail.

I walked out into the hallway and ran into Jeanette, and—oh my God—Ty was with her. What was he doing here?

Then I knew. He'd blown off his San Francisco trip to be here with me.

My heart did its wow-this-is-too-good-to-be-true flutter.

I wanted to throw myself into Ty's arms and give him a big kiss, but held back since Jeanette was standing there. They exchanged a few more words, then she disappeared through the double doors into the stockroom.

Ty looked fabulous in a dark suit, snow white shirt, and ruby red necktie. He slid his arm around me and gave me a quick kiss.

"I can't believe you're here," I said.

"Duty calls," Ty said, opening the stockroom door for me.

Duty? That's what I was now? A duty?

I walked ahead of him through the stockroom to the loading dock—and stopped still in my tracks.

Christmas trees circled the receiving area, all decorated and sparkling with white twinkle lights. Long buffet tables covered with green cloths were filled with a vast assortment of food and drinks. Tables and chairs had been set up, featuring red linens and lighted-candle centerpieces.

The big doors were rolled up, and outside I could see two catering trucks. Servers in crisp white jackets, wearing red Santa hats, continued to bring dishes inside.

The store employees—looking as mystified as I felt—clung together in small groups, whispering. Luckily, everyone was too caught up in the moment to ask why I'd been chasing Alyssa through the store, or why the cops had showed up.

Ty joined Jeanette and some of the other department managers. I found Bella and Sandy.

"What's going on?" I asked.

"I guess it's got something to do with the contest," Bella said.

"Wow," Sandy said. "If this is what we get for coming in last, can you imagine what the first-place store won?"

"Everyone!" Jeanette called. "Please take a seat!"

We all scrambled into chairs.

"Let's hear it!" Jeanette said. "Ho-ho-Holt's for the holiday!"

Everyone—but me---cheered along.

Jeanette introduced Ty. He was an eloquent speaker and always sounded sincere. He launched into a thank-you to all the employees for their blah, blah, blah, and I drifted off. I snapped back to attention when he paused and drew a big breath.

"It's with great pleasure and appreciation," Ty said, "that I award first place honors in the children's charity contest to this store."

First place? *First place?* To *this* store?

A stunned silence fell over the employees, all of us frozen with what-the-heck looks on our faces. Then, finally, everybody broke into applause.

"Last night, we thought we knew which store was our contest winner—and it wasn't this store," Ty said, and grinned.

The employees chuckled along with him.

"But all of that changed this morning," he went on. "Two large donations came in, pushing this store into first place by a wide margin."

Everyone looked around, wondering who had worked the Christmas miracle that had pulled off the win for us.

"One person made this possible though extraordinary dedication to Holt's programs," Ty said.

Somebody who worked here had extraordinary dedication to *Holt's*?

"That person not only put this store in first place," Ty said, "but garnered the most donations of anyone in any store, in the history of the Holt's department stores."

There's always at least one kiss-ass at every job.

"It is my privilege and honor to announce that person is," Ty said, and paused for effect, "Haley Randolph."

Everybody's—I swear—everybody's mouth fell open—including mine.

"No way!" somebody called out.

"Are you sure?" someone else shouted.

Ty gave an I-can't-believe-it-either-shrug and said, "Haley has made all of you big winners today."

Applause erupted. The employees around me patted me on the back and shook my hand. Cheers went up.

"Great job, Haley," the big guy from Men's Wear said.

"I knew you'd pull off something at the last minute," a girl nearby said.

"Oh, Haley, you rock!" Sandy said.

"This is b.s.," Bella said, then gave me a huge smile. "But I'll take it."

Oh my God. I couldn't believe it. What donations? I hadn't gotten any donations. This had to be some humongous Corporate screw up.

Still, I figured they'd straighten it out sooner or later, so why not enjoy the moment?

I rose from my chair, smiling my mom's beauty-queen smile, executing the royal elbow-elbow-wrist-wrist crowd-wave the British had perfected so beautifully.

I sat down and the room quieted.

"Each employee will receive a three-hundred-dollar Visa gift card," Ty announced.

Oohs and aahs rose from the room.

"And Haley," he went on, "will receive an all-expense-paid, seven-day cruise."

Even though I was the only one who received the grand prize, everybody applauded, which was nice.

"Thank you all very much for your hard work and for supporting Holt's programs," Ty said. He gestured toward the buffet tables. "Please, help yourselves."

Everybody headed for the food. I made my way toward Ty.

"Congratulations, Haley," he said, nodding his head in approval.

This didn't seem like the best time to tell him I hadn't gotten any donations, so what could I say but, "Thanks."

Ty touched my arm and urged me away from the other employees. He leaned down and said, "Alton and Sable have never contributed to our charity drive before. You must have really talked it up at their party last night."

The Staffords had made a large donation? In my name?

Okay, that was weird.

"But this other corporate donation you got," Ty said, frowning. "I've never heard of them. Who is Jackson Blair, and what is Blair Group International?"

I gasped. Oh my God.

"Ty?" Jeanette called. "The photographer is ready when you are."

He looked back at me, and I said, "It's fine, go ahead."

"We want you in some of the shots," Ty said.

"Sure, just let me go fix my hair," I said.

Ty and Jeanette left. I whipped out my cell phone and texted Jack. A few seconds later, my phone rang.

"Are you ready for some good news?" he asked when I answered.

"I've got a question for you," I said.

"I'm outside."

I paused. "The store?"

"Looks like a nice party," he said.

I walked to the big loading bay doors and looked out. It was dark. Security lights burned softly. I spotted Jack's Land Rover.

"Meet me at the side of the building," I said, and hung up.

I glanced around, saw that Ty and Jeanette were busy on the other side of the stockroom, then skipped down the stairs and around the corner.

Jack pulled up and parked. He got out looking hot-private-detective-fabulous in jeans and a gray shirt.

"Brooke sends her love," he said.

That could only mean one thing.

"She got Hope back? Already?" I asked.

Jack gave me a modest smile.

"I paid the Staffords a visit first thing this morning," he said. "I showed them the video."

"They must have been so mad," I said.

He thought for a few seconds. "I think 'foolish' best describes how they felt. They'd hired a security team. They thought they couldn't get caught. Then I presented them with proof that I—and that meant anyone—could walk into their home, expose what they were doing, and take that little girl away from them."

"The Staffords have so much money and power," I said. "That must have been a hard blow for them to accept."

"I think the possibility of a public scandal, a criminal indictment, and a civil lawsuit was uppermost in their minds," he said.

Jack had walked right into the home of a very wealthy, well-connected couple and pulled this off. It was so hot.

"So they gave Brooke's daughter back?" I asked.

"I drove her home immediately," he said.

I imagined the scene. Brooke, surprised, falling to her knees, screaming, crying, laughing, holding her little girl tight in her arms.

"It was ..." Jack cleared his throat. "Anyway, the Staffords promised to behave themselves in the future, and not cause any more problems with Hope."

"Like it matters," I said. "Brooke will never let them see her daughter again."

"Brooke is quite a woman," Jack said. "She still wants Alton and Sable to be a part of their granddaughter's life."

I didn't know if I could be that big-hearted.

"But no more sleepovers," Jack said. "Brooke knows this wouldn't have happened without your help. She said to tell you 'thanks,' and if you need anything—ever—to let her know."

"I'm just glad I could help," I said.

Then something popped into my mind.

"Is she planning to keep living in the house she and Chris bought?" I asked. "The one she mentioned, with the guest quarters out back?"

He shrugged. "As far as I know."

"I've got this friend. She's a really great person. She's desperately looking for a roommate," I said. "But I'm thinking that it would be better if she gave up her apartment, and Brooke could let her live in the guest quarters rent-free."

Jack considered it. "You'll vouch for her?"

"Heck, yeah," I said. "Her name is Jasmine Grady and she's going to be a fantastic actress."

"I'll call Brooke right away," Jack promised.

He nodded toward the store. "So you're the big winner in the contest, huh?" he asked.

"Thanks to you," I said. "You told Alton and Sable Stafford to make that big donation, didn't you?"

"They were anxious to make reparations," he said.   "I suggested it and they were happy to oblige."

Somehow, I doubted that was the full story, but I let it go.

"What about the donation from Blair Group International?" I asked.

He gave me a modest smile.

"You're still on my 'naughty' list," I said.

"'Naughty' is what I do best," he said.

My knees wobbled a little

"It was nice of you to make the donation for the children's charity," I said.

"But?" Jack asked, leaning toward me a little, like he knew I had something else on my mind—which I did, but it didn't suit me that he could read me so easily.

"But what you really wanted was that Breathless handbag," Jack said. "You know, Santa is watching. Have you been a good girl this year?"

"Not really," I said.

Jack grinned. He reached inside his Land Rover and pulled out a blue gift bag.

"Merry Christmas," he said.

All my senses jumped to high alert. My heart rate sped up. My breathing quickened.

"You didn't." I said that really quietly.

Jack kept grinning.

"Did you?" I might have yelled that.

He gave me a little see-for-yourself shrug.

"Did you?" I'm pretty sure I screamed that.

I couldn't stand it. I grabbed the gift bag, ripped out the tissue paper, and looked inside.

Light beamed down from above, and—I swear—angels started singing. Really.

I lifted a Breathless satchel, in all its buttery red leather glory, out of the bag.

Oh my God. It was gorgeous. Perfect. Exactly what I wanted.

"Thank you." I screamed that really loud.

I probably should have hugged Jack, but I clutched the Breathless in my arms instead—which, really, was for the best.

"I have to lock this in the trunk of my car," I said.

I couldn't take it back inside to the party with Ty in there—not that I intended to keep a secret from my official boyfriend, but still, timing in life was crucial and tonight simply wasn't the moment to mention it.

"I'll give you a lift," Jack said.

I hopped into his Land Rover and he drove around to the front of the store where my car was parked. I didn't have my purse with me, but I always kept a key in one of those little magnetic boxes in case of emergency.

Jack pulled up next to my Honda and I got out.

A huge sense of relief came over me. Not only had I gotten the fabulous Breathless satchel of my dreams and won a seven-day cruise, but all the bad stuff I'd been dealing with lately had been resolved.

The whole McKenna murder investigation was behind me. No more talking to suspects and hunting for clues. No more suspecting nice people of doing something horrible. And—thank goodness— no more Trent Daniels.

The Summer Santa Sale was over and done with. The store employees were speaking to me again. No more elf costume, no more ho-ho-Holt's-for the holidays, no more asking for donations—not that I'd done that, but still.

I circled the front of my Honda to get my key from under the fender and I noticed something stuck under my windshield wiper blade. It looked like a flyer, one of those advertisements for a free oil change or a new nail shop.

Then I noticed that it wasn't a piece of paper. It was an envelope.

Okay, that was weird.

I pulled it out from under the wiper blade and opened it.

A photo was inside.

My weird feeling got weirder.

I pulled it out.

It was a picture of me. I'd never seen it before.

How crazy was that?

In the photo I was standing on a sidewalk outside an apartment building. A man was standing next to me. I was gazing up at him with a serious look on my face.

Jeez, where had this thing come from? I'd never—

Then it hit me.

Oh my God. That was Trent Daniels' apartment building. And the guy I was gazing up at was—*him*.

Trent had Photoshopped us into the picture together.

Oh, crap.

Dear Reader,

There's more Haley out there! If you enjoyed this novella, check out the five full-length novels in the series. All of them are available from Kensington Books in hardcover, paperback, and eBook formats.

HANDBAGS AND HOMICIDE (first in the series)
Haley's life goes from glam to grim when she's forced to take a job at Holt's Department Store, and discovers her boss dead in the stockroom.

PURSES AND POISON (second in the series)
Haley substitutes for a sick waiter at a Holt's luncheon only to realize she's served the fruit arrangement that poisoned her boyfriend's ex.

SHOULDER BAGS AND SHOOTINGS (third in the series)
Life is going great for Haley—until she discovers her rival in the purse party business dead in the trunk of the Mercedes she borrowed from her boyfriend's grandmother.

CLUTCHES AND CURSES (fourth in the series)
When an irate Holt's customer puts a curse on Haley, she escapes to Las Vegas to help prepare a new store for its grand opening, and discovers her high school rival dead in a dressing room. Has the curse followed her, or what?

TOTE BAGS AND TOE TAGS (fifth in the series)
Haley lands a fabulous job at a major corporation in downtown Los Angeles only to find the chief of security, who's doing Haley's background investigation, dead in her office. Hot private detective Jack Bishop must help Haley solve the murder—but at what cost?

More information is available at www.DorothyHowellNovels.com and at my Dorothy Howell Novels fan page on Facebook. Follow me on Twitter @DHowellNovels.

Thanks for giving the Haley Randolph series a try!

Dorothy